A GUILTY WOMAN

CHARLOTTE BARNES

BLOODHOUND
BOOKS

THE MAINE MURDER MYSTERY CHANNEL
EPISODE 238

Release date: May 2015

Billy: Hello, loyal listeners, and welcome to another episode of *The Maine Murder Mystery Channel,* coming in with a special episode for you all this month because...

Liv: Because we've got a live one!

Billy: That's right, folks, we've got a live one. [Laughter] Well, maybe a *live* one isn't the best way of phrasing it.

Liv: An ongoing one?

Billy: Sure, an ongoing one seems fair.

Liv: What Billy is trying to say is that, instead of covering a cold case or a case that's already been wrapped up neatly for everyone, we've got the luxury of coming in *live* in the middle of a story that's only just unfolding.

Billy: If you're local to the area – actually, even if you're *not* local to the area – it's probably a case that you're already familiar with. News coverage around this one has been *next level* since the crime took place, and there's no signs of it slowing down.

Liv: Not surprisingly, given that a) it's a crazy crime and b) we still don't know why the hell it happened. We only know the where and the who, so that's going to have to be our focus for today.

Billy: Along with some wild speculation from us–

Liv: There will be no *wild* speculation, Billy, we're literally going to cover the details. Starting with the where, am I right?

Billy: Right? Right. So, settle in and let me set the scene for you guys. We're taking a tour through sunny Maine [laughter] and checking our bags at the Hotel Chrillon...

CHAPTER ONE

MARCH 2015

By the time my mother was making her first cup of tea of the day, I was on my third coffee. I knew it was her even before I checked the caller ID; maybe even before the phone rang. She called like clockwork on this day. I carried my coffee with me to grab the phone, then I went back to my armchair that overlooked the garden, pulled my legs up under me, and inhaled a breath so deep anyone would think there was a cigarette attached to the end of it.

'Mum.'

'Oh, love, I didn't think that you were going to answer. Have I... Is it a bad time?'

I thought of saying yes. I thought of saying yes and going back to my coffee and my quiet, and my deliberately free day. I never wanted to do anything on this day other than maybe head down to the coast. Thank God that Dad had been considerate enough to die at a time when dolphins were most visible. But because I am a good daughter, I didn't say yes. I didn't put the phone down and swallow the dregs of my drink, nor did I throw on a winter coat, pull my car out of the drive and head to the nearest coastal carpark. Instead, I pulled in another of those deep inhales and wondered why I'd decided to quit smoking at the same time as going through a divorce.

'Not at all, I was hoping you'd call.'

She loved to hear this. Since I moved out of grabbing distance and paved my way to the States, Mum's claws had dug in that bit deeper. I think she believed that emotional neediness might compensate for not being able to turn up on my doorstep whenever the idea struck her, but the two things didn't balance out. Still, being a good daughter meant allowing these things to happen.

'How are you feeling, hun, you doing okay?'

'I'm fine, Mum,' I paused to sip my drink, 'how are you?'

'Oh, you know.'

It's a quality of getting older that people find a way of telling you something is wrong without telling you what it is. There were times when Mum would call me to tell me she felt unwell, and when I asked how, or in what way, she would say, 'I just feel terrible,' as though feeling terrible were symptomatic of something. 'Oh, you know,' was another one of these party lines. She wasn't okay, but she wasn't going to tell me the particulars of it.

'I know it's hard without Dad,' I said then, cracking the seal on the topic of conversation that we would inevitably arrive at. 'I miss him, too.'

I said this annually, though I wasn't sure I ever said it during the months in between. His birthday went unacknowledged, as though the day he died trumped anything that happened while he was alive – including his birth itself. There were birthdays of my own, when I was younger, when I might say that I wished he were there. But I wasn't sure whether that was the same as missing him. There were things I missed about having a dad, but again, I wasn't sure–

'Your Aunt Gwen called last night, just to check in.' My

mother yanked the thought out at the root and I was back in the room. 'She asked to be remembered to you.'

'She's always welcome to call,' I lied. She wasn't welcome to call, but it was an easy thing to say given that Mum knew, and I knew, and Gwen probably knew, too, that there was no way she would ever pay the expense of a phone call to the States – and there was no way she was tech-savvy enough to download WhatsApp and call for free. If I'd known that moving over here would rid me of so much extended family, then I might have made the trip sooner. Dad's side was made up of cheapskates and Mum's side wasn't made up of much at all. She was an only child with two dead parents. I never met either of them, but I'd heard a lot about them. My mother inherited her knack for emotional manipulation from her mother, from what I'd heard, and I always wondered whether it was threaded into the DNA; whether there was a bright yellow strand of something running through our cores, whether that meant it was inevitable that that trait would catch up with me. There were times when I wondered whether it already had.

'Have you heard from Peter today, hun?'

I cough-spluttered as though something were lodged in my throat. 'Why would I have done?'

'I just thought...' There was a long and weighty pause while Mum tried to work out what exactly she'd been thinking when she asked. I wondered whether she regretted asking the question at all. I imagined her sitting in the living room, glancing over her shoulder, checking for the angles at which she might back her way out. 'I just thought he might reach out, that's all.'

'Peter and I have been divorced for five years, Mum. I don't think... I don't think he's obliged to remember Dad's anniversary anymore, and even if he does–'

'What about Joel, did he call?'

Ah, the more recent of my ex-husbands.

'No, Mum, he didn't call.'

'Honestly, that man, after you followed him—'

'I did not *follow...*' I let the sentence crumble in my mouth.

It didn't matter how many times I told her otherwise. Mum would always believe that I'd followed Joel out here in a bid to save our marriage. But by then our marriage had already started to deconstruct. I kept the loose parts of it in a shoebox that I brought over here with me, although I neglected to declare it at customs lest they refuse me a green card. Joel and I had met when he was technically working in London, but he was on a boys' weekend in Birmingham with people from his company. He was a financial accountant, working with a US firm that had merged with a UK one, and they'd agreed to a wife swap of employees. When I first saw him, he was leaning up against a bar and wincing over a pint of pale ale that a UK employee had encouraged him to try. Of course, it had been lust at first sight. We were married within minutes and separated within in hours. But somewhere between those points, his company had recalled him to the stateside office and I had agreed to go with him. I could have gone home to the motherland when everything went wrong, but I chose not to. Mum had never said as much, but I knew she held it against me.

'I didn't follow him out here, Mum,' I said again then, using my inside voice. 'It was time for a change and Joel gave me the opportunity for one.'

'You always say that, hun, that time for a change thing and I don't... I don't know...'

'I was restless.'

'You were grieving.'

'Grieving what?' I snapped. Dad had been dead for nearly ten years by the time I left. Peter and I had been divorced for three. The only thing I might have been grieving for was my twenties. 'Maybe I really did just need a change.'

'Okay, hun.'

'Will you see Dad today?'

Somehow, this change of subject felt safer. I leaned forward and set my empty cup on the window ledge in front of me while Mum thought about her answer, even though we both already knew what it would be.

'It's too upsetting, I can't... Do you think I should?'

'You don't have to visit his grave, Mum. You can remember him just as easily still.'

'You're right, no, I know you're right.' There came another pause that I didn't elect to fill. She would buy flowers, I thought, and then in an echo of that thought she added, 'I might go and get some tulips, or daffodils. He liked those.'

The man had steadfastly refused to ever buy my mother flowers owing to his firm belief that they were a waste of money. I smiled. 'That's a really good idea.'

'Will you call this weekend?' she asked, signalling the end.

'Sure, Mum, I'll give you a call.'

'Saturday or Sunday?' she pushed.

'Saturday. I'll call on Saturday.'

'I love you, hun.'

My throat was dry. It was the type of dryness that comes from exercising first thing in the morning, without water beforehand, maybe after a humid evening. I tried to swallow and felt a scratch like rough skin between my vocal folds.

'I love you too, Mum.'

'Take care, Caroline. Bye now.'

'Bye,' I answered, my voice quiet. She'd already gone.

CHAPTER TWO

The house was ripe with the smell of cooking, which I hated. I'd never been a big eater. My appetite had always been in proportion to my happiness, and in my adult life alone I'd lost a parent and two husbands, so I reasoned there was plenty to be miserable about. It was laziness sometimes, too, that starved my hunger; an innate inability to want to take care of myself. But when I had company, the option was so often taken away from me. And on this quiet Sunday lunchtime, the house still stank of pancake batter, fruit and fresh coffee, and I had to let myself be cared for. I didn't mind the coffee so much.

Noah was trailing lines across my stomach, a pattern recognisable only to him as though he were branding me somehow. I was trying to concentrate on breathing through my mouth while I played with his hair. It was something he'd told me he liked, which I took to be his way of asking me to do it more often.

'I love your stomach,' he said, speaking into the soft skin between my breasts.

'That's nice,' I answered, because he would be expecting an

answer. But truthfully, what do you say to a man when he's taking the time to compliment the part of yourself that you hate the most?

We'd spent part of the morning and most of the night before having sex. Noah had realised early on that the only way he would get an invitation for a full evening together was if I were to pass out from misadventure before I had the chance to ask him to leave. I was pretty sure he'd taken it upon himself to wear me out some evenings just so he didn't have to drive home. We'd woken early, drifting out of sleep in sync, and we found each other's bodies in the process. Noah was always hungry after a climax. Earlier that morning, he'd thrown on jeans and a shirt and disappeared to buy everything he needed to make pancakes. I'd stayed at home and stared out of my living room window, not smoking. I'd managed two pancakes before I'd taken him back to bed, and now we were here, him complimenting my stomach and me wondering how to ask him to leave.

Noah and I met within weeks of me and Joel un-meeting. Joel was already living in an apartment complex by then, one that had "bachelor" written all over the front of the building. Meanwhile, I found myself living alone. I told Noah that I wasn't looking for anything serious, which was why I'd chosen someone nearly ten years younger than me. But with the typical maturity of someone ten years younger than me, Noah seemed to take that remark as an invitation to try to change my mind. Our grand romance started with me bringing him home and having sex with him before asking whether he needed me to call him a taxi. He'd laughed and said he'd walk. It turned into a semi-regular affair after that. I didn't want to date him, but I have to admit that I was drawn in by the prospect of cocktails and dinner with a man who was very obviously my junior, and very obviously smitten. Though I'd still periodically reminded him that this wasn't intended to be a serious thing, and he'd nodded like he understood, even though I knew he didn't. But we'd fallen into a comfortable rhythm of regular sex and once-a-week drinks, to cater to everyone's needs, and during our last "big talk" about it all – something his therapist of all people had advised – I'd reminded him *again* that this was all it was ever intended to be. He'd still proposed three times since then; once in jest, twice in earnest. The first time made it impossible to take the second two seriously.

'What are you thinking about?' he asked me, pulling me back into the now.

I thought the question should have been my line. Isn't that what women are always asking of men: What are you thinking? Tell me what's on your mind?

'Nothing.'

Noah laughed. 'That's a big fat lie.' He craned his head around to face me. 'You're always thinking something, in that busy old brain of yours.'

I didn't resent the use of the word "old". It would do him good to be reminded of our age difference, and the inevitable difference in our needs that came with it.

'Sometimes,' I tapped his forehead twice, softly, 'it's completely empty in there.'

He laughed again and struggled to sit upright in bed, his back resting against his pillows now. Noah tucked an arm around me in an awkward invitation for me to cuddle into him, which I quietly declined by not moving.

'Then I must be doing something right.'

I liked that he wasn't offended by the cold shoulder. Though I disliked that there were times when, if anything, he seemed encouraged by it.

'What's your plan for today?' I asked, my way of letting him know that he didn't have plans with me. I felt Noah shrug. 'Are you working anywhere?'

Noah's career couldn't be considered high-powered by anyone's standards – but then, neither could mine. He was a glorified repair man and gardener, though when we'd met he referred to himself as a "landscaper". It meant that his working hours were dictated by the seasons and the weather conditions which, in Maine, were changeable at best. Still, he made a decent enough living; decent enough for a car and a house that he could afford to pay his bills on. And given that I wasn't likely to strap him into a plane seat and take him home to meet Mum at any point in the near future, I couldn't put too much weight into his lack of ambition. Joel had wanted the world on a platter with someone to dab a napkin to his lips for him when he'd finished devouring it, and look where that had got me.

'I'm meant to be meeting the boys to shoot a few rounds of pool later.'

'That'll be fun.'

He grumbled. 'Wanna come with me?'

'Absolutely not.' I turned and swung my legs out of bed. Noah ran a single fingertip down my spine and I shuddered at the contact. 'Sundays are for quiet.'

'I thought Sundays were for sex.' I didn't need to turn to know his expression; I could hear the grin on him. 'Speaking of...'

I stood up before Noah could get a hold of me, and I grabbed the nearest item of clothing I could find – which just so happened to be a college sweatshirt of Noah's that he still hadn't grown out of, in size, in stature, in maturity.

'You look hot in my clothes,' he said when I turned around.

'Do you want coffee?'

Noah laughed, but it wasn't a sincere sound. There was

something sad about it that caught my attention. 'I swear to God, Caroline, sometimes I wonder whether you even like me.'

'You're fishing for compliments.'

'I am not! I'm fishing for... affirmation. It's a love language.'

I narrowed my eyes at him. 'You've been talking to your therapist about me again.'

'So what if I have?'

'So help me,' I tugged on a pair of jogging bottoms to go with the jumper, 'you bloody Americans and your therapists.'

'You bloody Brits and your pent-up attitude to everything.' He tried to say the sentence in a mock British accent, but it sounded too slapstick. It was a great American pastime, I'd learned since moving here, mocking the British accent. 'Seriously, if you like me, and we get along, which we clearly do,' he indicated the mess of bed sheets, 'why doesn't this ever become more serious, huh? Answer me that. Why don't you just agree to marry me already?'

I choked on a laugh. 'There are a few steps between more serious and marriage.'

'So I skipped ahead.'

I started to walk towards the door. 'Skip ahead to your truck. I've got work to do.'

'On your *novel*?'

He leaned so hard on the word that I could practically hear the air quotes around it.

'Don't start something you can't finish, Noah.'

'Jesus, Caroline, can...' The sentence petered out and he sighed. I was facing away from him still, and I wasn't about to turn back into the room, not when I was so close to getting out of it. 'Can I at least see you this week?'

'I've got two days at the paper and two days at the college.'

'And what about the fifth day?'

'That's to work on my *novel*.'

I used the same mocking tone that he had, and then I left, heading for the bathroom. By the time I'd finish showering he was in the kitchen making an early lunch: all was forgiven. Noah was a good kid, really. He just let me get away with too much.

CHAPTER THREE

The older I got, the more time I spent trying to get into character.

My writing day started with a drive out to Acadia National Park. The deeper I got into the new book, the more physical space I needed to let the story spread out. I imagined it now as an over-sized toddler, kicking and throwing its limbs in the hope that it might hit something. At least in an open space this size, the worst thing it would hit would be a rock face or some foliage, rather than a wall or a door. I locked the car and took one of the paths most travelled because I wasn't exactly the rock climbing type. It was one of those things that I'd idly fantasised about when Joel invited me to the States; I made it sound as though it had always been a dream for me to gear up and launch myself at something I could fall from. Though realistically, I'd had plenty of opportunities for it back home and I'd always managed to resist the temptation.

'Beautiful morning for it, isn't it?'

A voice caught me off-guard and I turned sharply, in time to catch a couple who were suited with water bottles and tight shorts.

'It really is,' I answered.

'Are you visiting?' the man asked, clocking my accent, I guessed.

'No, I moved over here a while ago.'

'Haven't picked up the Maine twang yet, then?' the woman chimed in.

I forced a laugh. 'Not yet, but give me time.'

'It'll catch up with you eventually,' she joked.

'I've no doubt about it.' *Everything does*, I thought with a tight smile. 'You have yourselves a good day now.'

'And you, happy climbing.'

'You might want to grab some water from one of the pit-stops,' the man added, and I thought, thank God that a man was here in the nick of time to tell me that I might need to hydrate at some point.

I had a protein bar and a small water bottle in my backpack along with my notebook and lucky pen. Lucky, because I had already managed to plan three novels with it. Although, given that none of the books had skyrocketed to the giddy heights of commercial success, anyone could be forgiven for wondering how lucky the pen was after all.

I'd written the first book after Dad died. It was a tortured stream of consciousness about a woman who helped her husband to commit suicide after a long-standing battle with cancer. No one could accuse me of being light-hearted in my subject matter. Mum had accused me of borrowing too heavily from real-life in my writing, stealing from something that should have remained private.

'Dad didn't have cancer, Mum, only depression,' I'd snapped back during the argument, and I remember thinking, *now that would be good dialogue for a story.*

The novel was picked up by a small independent publisher back home. I hadn't known enough about the industry to even know what a literary agent was at the time; I was just delighted by the interest. I was a naïve schoolgirl (metaphorically speaking, that is) who'd turned the head of someone older, wiser; someone who could get my book into Waterstones, which was all that mattered at the time. Imagine my disappointment when every Waterstones I went into, searching out my surname in the alphabetised fiction stock, left me empty-handed and down-hearted. It was the classic love story of a young woman drawn in by the empty promise of something more. But like every failed relationship, I at least learned something from that book – and I didn't work with the same publisher a second time.

I perched on a smooth rock formation and looked out over the landscape. America might have had its problems, but I'll be damned if it didn't have some views that made up for it. I pulled in greedy amounts of clean air and enjoyed every exhale like it was something addictive; maybe it was, in its way. These trips to the park had become a near weekly occurrence. On the writing days when I wasn't here, I was right on the outline of the coast instead. The ease of access to beaches, bay sides and tall-standing nature spots made Maine worth staying in. I like to think it made writing easier, too, but I'm not all that sure it did. My second novel had been written mostly in mine and Peter's back bedroom – the bedroom that he had wanted to redecorate as a nursery, and I'd insisted on keeping as an office space. I joked, once, that I was birthing something in there, in my own way, but he hadn't laughed. That's probably when I realised that we were doomed – and that marrying someone straight out of university is a terrible idea. Still, that second novel came easier than the first, and that was something to be thankful for.

Back then, on the days when I wasn't teaching, or writing something for someone else to teach, I was working on the novel. For hours at a time I would chip away at a story about a woman who, after an argument with her husband, went out for a late night drive to clear her head, only to hit someone hitchhiking on a country road. The story followed her for the stretch of time afterwards, saw a slow descent into worry and guilt as she covered up the crime and spent her days trying to outrun any trace of it. It ruined her marriage, but at least she got away with killing someone, which an agent – because I knew what an agent was by then – told me was a nice ending. He found a publisher for the work; bigger than the last, but not quite big enough for Waterstones. My first royalty cheque covered my share of the mortgage for that month though, and I remember gleefully waving the figures under Peter's nose by way of saying, look, look, I've made something better than a baby. He still didn't agree. He cared for my writing even less when I told him the idea for my third book: a teacher who's drawn into a world of small time drug deals at her local school, feeding on working class students who needed a hit to get them through the day.

'You'll never work in a school again if you write something like that,' he'd told me.

'Maybe I'll never *need* to work in a school again if I write something like this.'

It took longer for the third book; a lengthier gestation period, given that Peter left me during chapter two. My agent had told me to take my time with it, and so I had. I'd taken a divorce, several drinking binges, a lost job and two extra stones in weight.

'It's too slow, honey, too slow,' my agent had said when I gave him the first draft.

In the revised version, two students overdosed from drugs supplied by the teacher. That fixed things.

'You'll get a numb butt if you stay like that for too long.'

Another voice; another interruption. I looked up and caught sight of an offensively attractive man wearing climbing gear – water bottle and all.

'I never stay in the same place long,' I answered.

'I suppose there's plenty to see around these parts, isn't there?' He smiled. I couldn't place his accent, but it was clear he wasn't from here – wasn't from the States, even – and that made me warm to him faster. 'Planning a hike?'

I laughed. 'I'm not exactly geared for it.'

'No,' he paused and gave me a deliberate look over, 'what is it you're geared for?'

I was wearing worn out Converse pumps that once upon a time had been white, though they were now the type of grey that snow mounds turn when too many people have driven through them. I'd paired them with cut-off jeans and a loose-fit jumper with something written in French across the front even though I'd never spoken the language, or studied it, having opted for German instead. I liked the harsher sounds. My notebook was balanced on my knee, pen in hand.

'I'm geared for writing, I suppose.'

'You're an author?'

It was an ill-fitting name that I'd never felt comfortable with, but other people had always loved to use it.

'I suppose so.'

'Anything in print?'

'Sure,' I smiled, 'three novels. Crime, mostly.'

'Ah, what's your name? I'll look out for you.'

'Caroline Geel.'

'I'll look out for you then, Caroline Geel.' He dipped his head as though he was tipping a hat. 'I'll leave you to your...' He gestured to the notebook.

'Enjoy your climb,' I answered, before turning my attention back to the blank page.

Across the top of the page I wrote, *What if she's killed someone?* And I spent the next half an hour idly wondering, asking questions of the woman in the story, as though I wasn't even in control of the answers.

TRUE CRIME FEMINISTAS
EPISODE 54

Release date: May 2015

Hallie: Hello and welcome to another episode of *True Crime Feministas*, angels. We're your hosts, Hallie and...

Hayley: Hayley! And today we're talking about... Wait, Hall, what is it we're talking about?

Hallie: True crime and another middle-class white woman.

Hayley: [Laughter] That's right, listeners, once again the pendulum has swung back to the age-old chatter about white women and true crime.

Hallie: *Middle-class* white women; you need to get that right. If Caroline Geel was a working-class woman there's a damn fine chance that we wouldn't be having this conversation right now.

Hayley: Weeeeeeell, *we* probably would be. But other podcasts certainly wouldn't be.

Hallie: Fair, fair, I hold my hands up to that one. We would definitely have something to say about this, regardless of social class. But her social class definitely helps, am I right or am I right?

Hayley: Yes, you're painfully right.

Hallie: Which begs the question, what's so damn special about Caroline Geel?

CHAPTER FOUR

APRIL 2015

I was a qualified teacher, for what it was worth. After doing an English literature degree and then not quite knowing what to do with it – a tale as old as time – I trained to be a teacher, with Peter alongside me also training, but it was midway through that meddlesome journey that I started to idly flirt with journalism. Two postgraduate courses had seemed indulgent, so I pursued one and started to cheat with journalism on the side instead, taking extra jobs for the evenings and weekends, sending out pitches wherever I could think of. It drove Peter wild with frustration and that manifested in him frequently reminding me of the job I was actually working towards: teaching, allegedly. But nothing spurs on a stubborn woman quite like being told there's something she shouldn't be doing. Of course, I continued with both lines of work and now, upwards of ten years later, I barely had a foot in either industry. Since moving to the States I'd managed to pick up freelance work with a local print publication, where I covered what passed for crime stories. Without focussing on international news – which I was told more than once by my domineering boss was outside of my remit – that inevitably meant that many of my weekly writing assignments contended with car theft and sporadic spikes in drug sales; my students were sometimes responsible for both of those things.

'What the hell is this?' Karl lumped a balled-up piece of paper on the hot desk I was using that day. From the corner of my eye I could see he was wearing chinos with a stain on the crotch that I was desperate to point out but it didn't seem like the time. He'd separated from his wife last month, and he hadn't quite adjusted to taking care of himself yet; it was a hard feat for some adults. 'What am I meant to do with this?'

I wanted to suggest recycling it, but I also had a strong suspicion that the balled-up lump he'd just thrown at me was in fact the article I'd thrown at him the day before. It was an interview with Carrie Watson, a local mother whose daughter had died in a hit and run car crash five years ago, and we were nearing the anniversary of her accident. I wrote it as a commemorative piece to document the woman's lived tragedy and highlight the ongoing spate of unsolved deaths by car collision in the wider state.

'What the fuck am I meant to do with it, Geel?' he asked again when I didn't answer. I was trying to think of something smart to say, but I'd been awake for nearly twelve hours and I was running on two coffees and a slice of toast. No one in the office included the freelancers in their coffee or food runs.

'I thought it was crime meets human interest,' I answered flatly. I was speaking to the corner of my laptop rather than to him, and I knew that would annoy him. Still, I wouldn't give him the satisfaction of looking at him while he towered over me. I wasn't stupid enough not to realise what he was doing by refusing to take the empty seat on the other side of my workspace. But he wasn't the sort of man I could bring myself to look up to. 'It's been a slow week in the local area and I thought–'

'What about those kids that were caught joyriding?'

Oh good, I thought, another car theft to write about.

'I don't know that I can stretch that to a page.'

'Well, this,' he flicked the ball of paper so it tumbled off my desk, landing somewhere by my feet, 'isn't going to fill a page in this paper. If you're struggling for ideas then either talk to one of the regulars and see what they've got cooking, or we can turn the space over to someone else. Do you wanna turn the space over to someone else?'

'No.'

'Then learn how to play with others. Talk to Truman; he's got some ideas brewing.'

'Sure thing, Karl, I'll get right on that,' I answered, talking to the miniature version of him that I imagined standing on the corner of my laptop, stamping his feet, arms crossed, eyebrows tight together. He was the size of my pinkie's fingernail.

'So help me...' he muttered as he walked away.

Alongside adding to Karl's recycling contributions, another one of my weekly tasks was to edit the work of other writers before it went to print. The irony was bittersweet in the bowl of my tongue that I was midway through red-penning an article of Truman's as Karl walked away from me. I thought it would at least give me some ground, a lofty perch even, to have handy when I crawled over to Truman's desk and asked what local news he had that I could pilfer and edit into something that read like crime. I'd long wondered whether part of the reason Karl was so severe when it came to his judgement of my work was that he simply didn't want to acknowledge that local crime was a thing. There were a lot of residents in these parts who felt like that. It didn't look good on the place, especially a hotspot so close to tourist attractions, and with national parks and beaches dotted around the state; the last thing anyone in a position of authority might want to admit was that visitors shouldn't leave valuables in their cars. But if they wanted to buy poor quality drugs then they'd probably come to the right place.

That, and Karl just didn't like me.

'Fancy a coffee?' Truman spoke over the top of my laptop. I narrowed my eyes and felt my head tilt, an involuntary reaction, and he laughed. 'There aren't any hidden strings, Geel. Jesus, I'm just offering you a coffee. I need to stretch my legs.'

'Okay,' I saved what I was doing, 'a coffee would be good.'

Truman and I took a silent wander down the street to the local coffee spot where the other journalists took their breaks. The place was dead when we walked in though, everyone too busy rushing towards their daily deadlines before an acceptable time to clock off rolled around. He offered to buy, but I didn't want him to have the leverage, so I insisted it was my treat. Because Truman is a living and breathing mess of clichés, he asked for an espresso – but he pronounced it with an "x" because he's also a heathen.

'Dig in,' I said, setting the drink in front of him.

'What d'you get?' He nodded towards my mug. 'Tea?'

I laughed. 'Because I'm British and all I drink is tea.'

'Well, yeah.'

'No,' I blew across the steam of my latte and aimed the coffee scent at him, 'I need something stronger than that. Besides which, your tea here is terrible.'

'It's not what we're known for. And you'll never really be one of us until you own a gun,' he said then, albeit in a joking tone. Of course, I did own a gun. It came free with my divorce and my right to remain in the country. Truman fidgeted with the corner of a napkin and then looked out the window as he spoke. 'I heard Karl riding your ass again earlier.'

'One of his favourite pastimes.'

'Well...' Truman petered out and I wondered what the end

of the sentence might be. Whatever it was, he clearly didn't have the stones to say it. 'He tell you to pick my brains?'

'Doesn't he always? Tell me, how does it feel to be the blue-eyed boy?'

Truman laughed and stared down at the table. There was a pale pink flush moving up one of his cheeks. 'It isn't like that.'

'Okay, we don't have time for me to pander to that. What do you have?'

He laughed again; the sound erupted out of him and his eyes widened, as though he was surprised by the noise. 'You don't waste any time do you, Geel?'

'Was this meant to be a social coffee?' I asked, knowing the answer. There was nothing social about my dealings with the permanent staff. I was on the fringes. 'You scratch my back, so on and so forth. There's obviously something you want, too.'

'Maybe I just wanna help, d'you ever think of that possibility?' *No.* 'Maybe I'm actually a good guy, Geel, that ever cross your mind?' *Also no.*

I sipped my drink. 'I'm sorry, it's been a long... I want to say day.'

'The piece of mine you're editing,' he started and I felt myself relax. There *was* something he wanted. 'D'you get to the part where I quote the woman from the opposing party yet?'

'The part where she says the opposition are a likely threat against her campaign?'

'Mm,' he murmured, 'I need you to change the quote.'

'To what?' I asked, as though the request didn't bother me. But I understood the implications of it.

'Be creative. Something about the opposition not standing a chance.'

'But that isn't what she said?'

Truman looked straight at me then, through eyes that were now slim slits. I wondered whether he could see me at all, his expression had tightened so much. 'I need you to change the quote,' he said again and this time I only nodded. 'Okay.' He took a sip of his drink and winced, then leaned across the table to lessen the distance between us. He spoke in a lowered tone, as though he were about to swap something that was worthy of what he'd asked me to do. 'Now I'll tell you about the cattle that those joyriding kids mowed down during their little trip around the houses...'

This is my fucking crime story?

CHAPTER FIVE

Alongside being a lapsed journalist, I also found the time in the average week to be a lapsed teacher. I covered classes at the local high school on a temporary, hourly paid contract that could be cut short at a moment's notice, regardless of the lesson prep that had been put into my week. The cancellations didn't happen often, admittedly, but they still happened. Then there were the times when the opposite of a cancellation occurred, and instead of a dearth of work there was a flood of it that could only be described as biblical. Unfortunately, that also meant–

'Connor, get the hell down from that high rope.'

'Sorry, Miss Geel!'

They would expect me to cover all manner of hellish subjects, including Physical Education – or Gym Class, as it was otherwise known – and Math, which was a bellyache reminder of Peter, who would spend hours torturously studying his syllabus for the week ahead, searching for ways to make it interesting to his students. The only way to make maths interesting, I'd always thought, was to disguise it as another subject entirely; it was an input that Peter had never warmed to, and perhaps another nail in the proverbial coffin that buried us both alive. The fact that neither had any respect for what the other one did, or wanted to do, with their lives. We were an ugly and flawed pairing if ever there was one, but at least the thought of us both having met the loves of our lives during university and married straight out of it had kept our parents happy for a while. I'd always thought the divorce was more harmful to the mental health of our families than it had been to ours.

I blew hard on the whistle to signal a five-minute warning for the end of class. I'd spent much of the last hour watching young bodies dart from one side of the room to the other, all the while pretending to keep an eye on the young men who doubled as chimps and insisted on an in-class dick measuring as to who could touch the ceiling by climbing the high rope. I took a pathetic pleasure in making sure none of them ever got close.

'Connor, what did I just say?'

'Sorry, Miss Geel.'

'Sorry, Miss Geel,' another boy echoed in a mocking tone and I cocked an eyebrow at him. I didn't have much authority as a roll-in teacher, but there's something to be said for the power of a judgemental look from an older woman when you're a young man learning that that thing between your legs isn't just to piss out of. 'Sorry, Miss Geel,' the same boy said again then, his tone more sincere and his head slightly stooped as though he'd been given an actual reprimand.

'I want you showered, dressed and out of my changing room within a quarter of an hour,' I shouted to the room, and the instruction was met with slow murmurs of agreement.

One young woman separated herself from the pack. She took laboured steps towards me, killing time for the room to clear. It had nearly emptied of students by the time she drew to a stop in front of me and asked, 'Miss Geel, can I go to the nurse's office? I...' She looked down and scuffed one shoe against the other. 'I need to go to the nurse's office.'

'Period?' I asked, and her face flushed a matching colour. It wasn't just to embarrass her, although I didn't hate that part of it. It was because I wanted young women to move away from a culture of hiding tampons up their sleeves, and I was making that change one embarrassed and shamed girl at a time. If I'd had one on me, I would have pulled it out and waved it in the air before handing it to her. 'Take your time,' I added when she didn't answer, and she skulked away.

After ten minutes I started to round up the creatures in the girls' changing rooms; a space that was a mess of hairspray and compact powder as students hurried to put their appearances back together after an hour of mild sweating. I wondered whether there was a way to measure hormones and, complementary to that, I imagined a thermometer style device fixed to the wall of the room, something like mercury rising to the roof of the measuring stick the longer the girls spent in the space.

'Come on, class beckons,' I said as the last few lingered by their lockers still.

The boys' changing room wasn't my terrain, and I'd never been sure of what authority I even had in entering there. But I knew that there would be young men in there, too; probably also with hairspray and compact powder, putting themselves back together.

'Coming in,' I said with three firm knocks on the door. Coach Western, if he'd been here, absolutely would have gone into the girls' changing room to yank students out. That's what I was telling myself when I trod into the steamed space, rank with sweat and trace amounts of testosterone.

It looked mostly empty, but I rounded a corner to find two boys still talking. I knew one of them as Elliot, but I didn't know the name of the other; there were too many students to name in a school like this. From the way they jumped apart I knew they were doing something they shouldn't be; from the fact they were both fully clothed I knew they couldn't have been doing *that*, which I probably would have let slide. But I took an educated guess at the other activities they might be trying to hide and landed on–

'Where is it?'

Elliot looked to the other boy, who shrugged. 'Where's what, Miss Geel?' Elliot asked.

'Can I get your name?'

The unknown male cleared his throat. 'Teddy.'

'Teddy,' I said, in an inappropriately soft tone, 'I don't know you all that well, so you'll forgive me for needing to ask. Are you selling or buying?'

'Miss–'

'Elliot, you can answer if you prefer, but I'd rather ask Teddy.'

Teddy wasn't nervous. He was the archetypal Cool Kid who often got caught doing things wrong and often didn't give much of a shit when it happened. He turned out his pockets and shrugged.

'I don't know what you're talking about, Miss Geel,' he answered, with a butter wouldn't melt expression. *It would probably fry.*

'Elliot,' I turned on the other boy, 'are you comfortable turning out your pockets?'

'I'd rather not, Miss.'

'Do you want to tell me why that is?'

'I'd rather not, Miss,' he parroted.

'Miss,' Teddy spoke up then, his tone relaxed, friendly even, 'it's just a treat to give Elliot a pick-me-up. Is there anything so wrong about that?'

I laughed; I couldn't help myself. The line was straight out of a poorly written B-movie and I wondered whether he'd actually borrowed it from one, maybe back-pocketed it for an occasion such as this when he could try it out on a teacher that he thought had no authority over him. *What a wrong assumption*, I thought as I closed the short distance between us. I stared hard at Teddy, but I held a hand out in Elliot's direction.

'There's a great deal that's wrong with it. Elliot,' the boy let out a noise of discomfort, as though I'd pinched him, 'I'm going to need whatever you've got in your pocket.'

There was a rustle as he removed the bag. He placed it in my palm.

'Miss,' I turned to look at Elliot as he spoke, 'what happens now?'

I weighed up the bag in my hand. It was only marijuana. If I'd been back home, there would have been uproar at a bag like this being passed around the school I used to teach at: a high-end private establishment packed with old money. Here, things were different.

'I'm going to have to report this, Elliot, and then it'll be up to Principle Deven what happens next. I'm sure he'll speak to you both in due course.'

'Miss–'

'You're late for your next class, Elliot. I suspect you are, too, Teddy?'

Again, the young man shrugged. 'Whatever, I guess. Come on, Elliot.'

'Yeah, go on, Elliot,' I mimicked Teddy's don't-give-a-shit tone.

The boys left with a shuffle and a murmur. I imagined Elliot hyperventilating as soon as they stepped out of the changing rooms. I imagined Teddy, probably going to his locker to retrieve another stash. And as I bounced the baggie up and down in my hand, I couldn't help but wonder who the kid's source was.

CHAPTER SIX

I had never been the woman who was friends with all the women. That's not to say that I didn't get along with women, any more or less so than men. But socialising never came easily to me. That is, until I got divorced – the first time. When Peter and I separated, the female partners of his male friends saw to it that I hardly had time to feel lonely – more's the pity, I remember thinking more than once – and that primed me for the friends I would make on my own, independently of Peter, down the line. Of course, all those friendships were abruptly severed when I met Joel, married him, and abandoned everyone I knew in favour of a stateside existence. I hadn't bothered to keep in touch; it had never occurred to me that it was a thing I should do. But since moving here, since nesting, there were a few women I'd managed to attach myself to, and they were enough to cater to my socialising quotas.

'Do you mind if I put the wine in the freezer?'

Beverley was a single mother of two, re-training from her former existence as a nursery nurse to be an actual nurse, and she could drink alcohol like it was chilled water. I'd seen the woman down two fingers of whiskey without wincing on the first night I met her, when we'd shamefully been drinking by ourselves in a bar, and from that moment I knew she and I would get along just fine.

'Can't you just put it in the fridge like a normal person?'

Annaliese was tamer, but she came free with Beverley so I had to keep her. She was a widow – her husband having died in a car accident involving a drunk driver two years ago – and was child-free. 'Not childless,' she'd stipulated when I first met her, and I hadn't realised until that very moment what a semantic split those two phrases caused. She worked at the local bank and, from what I'd seen, she had a fairly comfortable life. She didn't make huge amounts of money, but she didn't need to; she had a wide enough social circle; she had a family who she seemed close to. In short, she had all the right things, and she was simple enough to be blissfully satisfied by that.

'It'll just speed the process along, won't it?' Beverley answered. 'Shaz, what did you bring?'

'Myself.' Shaz was staring at her phone, leaning in the corner join of my kitchen worktops, and even in this slouched position she managed to look like a model. She was an administrative assistant at the local job agency, which is how she and I had met. Apparently, I'd dazzled her with my charming wit and sparkling personality when I'd told her what I was and wasn't prepared to do for a living. We'd swapped numbers, kept in touch, and I'd indoctrinated her by inviting her to Beverley's for dinner and drinks one evening, when it had been Beverley's turn to host. I'd thought having a younger woman there might somehow balance out Annaliese's beige-ness, maybe even make her slightly more interesting. Neither thing had happened, but Shaz and Beverley had got along well enough for her to form part of the group. And now here we were, a slightly mismatched foursome of grown women arguing about whether it was worth putting wine in the freezer or not.

'There's ice in the freezer, why don't you just add that?' I suggested while I shook a share packet of cheese balls across two bowls. No one could accuse me of not making an effort for my guests.

'Caroline, I swear, you Brits are strange as all hell but that is a genius plan.' Beverley knocked about in the freezer drawers until she found the ice tray. 'Ann, pass some glasses, would you?'

'Not for me, thanks,' Shaz said, and all three of us turned on her. She burst out laughing, in her young person's giggle that still had energy and happiness threaded through it. 'I'm kidding, obviously. Hit me.'

Beverley handed her a glass.

'Caroline?'

'Obviously.'

'Annaliese?'

'Only a small one. I don't want to feel like crap in the morning.'

'And anything more than a small one will do that?' Shaz asked, as though the concept were completely alien to her. She'd managed to hold this conversation all the while glued to the screen of her phone still, but then she tutted, locked the handset and slipped it into her back pocket.

'Let me live vicariously through you,' Beverley spoke to her while handing me a drink, 'what asshole are we tutting over this week?'

'Chad.' Shaz made it sound like a curse word.

'With a name like Chad, what do you expect?' I threw a packet of peanuts for Beverley to catch and then I balanced two bowls of cheese balls in the palm of one hand. 'Living room? We may as well get comfortable for whatever she's about to regale us with. Annaliese, could you...' I nodded towards a bowl of pretzels on the side.

'So, we met on this dating app, right?'

'Because all great romances start with a dating app,' Beverley interrupted her.

'Where else do you meet people now?' I asked.

Beverley let out a curt laugh that made my shoulders bunch up an inch. 'You seem to do just fine. How's Noah these days?'

'Ah, hello?' Shaz chimed in then and I was glad that she was pulling the attention back. I didn't want to talk to the women about Noah. It authenticated the relationship too much to have it in the open like that, and I always resisted the idea of doing that – for their benefit, as much as my own. I had too much lived experience of friends becoming invested or embroiled in relationships, only to be as deeply disappointed as the actual participants when everything came to an end. I'm sure that when Peter and I separated there were friends of ours that attended actual counselling sessions to contend with the news – our parents probably had done, too. Besides which, the relationship with Noah wasn't going to last long enough for it to be worth causing any emotional disturbance to friends of mine.

It took nearly forty minutes for Shaz to explain that the reason Chad was an asshole was because he swapped a few messages with her, arranged a date, and then didn't show up. It seemed like a love story I could have written in two sentences. Since then, he'd messaged her non-stop to explain that his car broke down in a signal dead zone, which is why he couldn't get in touch with her at the time, and she'd told us in four different ways why she thought that was a bullshit excuse.

'Thank you, next,' Beverley said as she threw a pretzel into her mouth. She swilled it down with another mouthful of wine. 'Honestly, men these days. You can't live with them...' She gestured with her glass and I watched flecks of liquid spill over the side. I imagined some spots of alcohol, maybe even Beverley's DNA, landing in the fibres of my carpet. 'That's probably the end of the sentence, to be fair.'

'That's not fair though,' Annaliese snapped and I leaned back in my armchair, let the pillows of it envelope me as I settled in for a diatribe about the beauties of human connection. 'Ethan and I were incredibly happy, so happy, and he...' Emotion lodged in her throat and she looked out of the window. 'He was a good man.'

Beverley leaned forward to squeeze her friend's hand. 'I know he was, sugar.' She let a beat of quiet pass before saying, 'Caroline, you're the host. Can you provide us with a subject change?'

I checked my watch and weighed up the possibilities. 'We should order pizza.'

'*That's* your subject change?' Shaz asked, affronted.

I leaned forward to the small wooden box that was resting on my windowsill. From inside I pulled out rolling papers and a squat bag of marijuana. 'Maine's finest,' I said as I threw it across to Beverley, who was wide-eyed with Christmas morning joy. 'Like I said, we should probably order pizza.'

'You order,' Beverley answered, 'I'm rolling.'

'I'll order,' Shaz already had her phone out, 'what's everyone having?'

'Vegetarian supreme,' I said.

Beverley had her nose buried in the bag like a Victorian starlet who'd been gifted smelling salts. 'Meat feast.'

'I won't have any, thank you.'

Shaz's head snapped around to look at Annaliese. 'You're not having pizza?'

'No, I'm not having,' she nodded at Beverley, 'I'm not having that.'

'Not even a smidge?' Beverley held her thumb and index finger up with a small gap between them. 'A taste? I'll bet Caroline worked really hard to get this for us.'

'I did,' I sipped my drink, 'it took me ages to confiscate that from a student.'

'Caroline!' Annaliese looked as though I'd slapped her around the face and I couldn't help but wonder how it might feel to actually do that one day.

'I'm joking, obviously.'

'Obviously...' Beverley echoed as she sprinkled weed along the length of a paper.

CHAPTER SEVEN

In two weeks I had added seventy-two words to the new book. The summer was nearing, and my self-imposed deadline of having a draft before the season was out was looking increasingly unlikely, the closer we crept towards May. I'd limited dealings with Noah to the weekends alone and I was taking on only what work I needed to, to survive comfortably. Of course, my idea of surviving comfortably now meant bribing myself with dinner for one at a local seafood restaurant – *if* I could get 1,000 words written that day. I was up to 862 when I found myself in my kitchen, pulling a middle-sized blade out of my knife block and weighing it up in my hand. *Could I kill someone with this?* I wondered as I bounced the handle and felt the weight of it thud down again. It hardly seemed like the easiest thing to manoeuvre. I jabbed the blade into the air in front of me, once, twice, before deciding, *No, this won't do at all*.

I put the knife back in the block and went back to my laptop. After the crucial act of staring at the wall for ten minutes, I wrote a paragraph wherein my main character wonders about the practicalities of killing someone with something poisonous. Then she wonders aloud whether this makes her mad, or whether, in wondering whether she's mad, she exhibits too much awareness of the possibility of madness, and whether in some ways, that negates the madness existing. And just like that, I'd written another 348 words. They were utter shit and I would delete all but 51 of them when the time came, but still.

'Fifty-one seems a touch generous even,' I said while I waited for the whir of my cloud storage to kick in. Once the document had uploaded, I slammed the laptop closed, turned the light off, and locked the door. I sometimes imagined my writing as a small demon that needed to be kept under wraps.

The seafood spot was a ten-minute walk from home, which was another tick in its favour. That, and every Thursday evening it lost clientele to a nearby bar that was hosting a quiz night and apparently my neighbours couldn't resist the pull. I had the pick of tables when I walked in and the waitress let me seat myself quietly, having gestured to the entire restaurant floor and handed me a menu.

'I'll give you a minute to browse.'

'Thanks,' I answered with a tight smile. She was new here. She didn't yet know that I ordered the same thing every week – the seafood combo with a gin and slimline tonic – which I guessed meant she didn't know I was now such a loyal customer that the owner often put it through at a discount: another tick in the restaurant's favour. But then, if you only have one customer on a particular evening, I suppose it pays to play extra nice with them. I browsed the menu idly in case I felt like surprising myself with something different, but no. The waitress took the cue of me folding the menu over and drumming my fingers on the table, and after scribbling down whatever shorthand she used for combo and a gin, she disappeared off with the promise of bringing my drink soon.

While dinner alone was a quiet joy – one I thought that

more people should afford themselves the luxury of – I still
brought company with me. I pulled *The Talented Mr Ripley* out
of my backpack. It wasn't my first time reading the book, but it
was my first time in a *long* time and it felt very much like mine
and Tom's first journey through Italy together. Each chapter left
me dumbfounded by the sheer balls on the character, the way in
which he tricked anyone who questioned him, the ways in
which he made himself anew. I admired and envied that in
equal parts. I wondered whether my own character might make
herself anew at some point during our story; whether murder
was going to do that for her, in the same way it seemed to do for
Tom. I reached down to my bag to feel my way around for a
pen, and I underlined an entire paragraph detailing the ways in
which his friend's clothes fit him. There was something
beautiful about that borrowing.

'One gin.'

I looked up in time to exchange a smile with the waitress.
'Thanks so much.'

'No problem, ma'am.'

Ma'am. I parroted and tried to still a shudder that
threatened to move through me.

I was two pages further into the story – another suit, another
act of trickery – when another interruption came. I was acutely
aware of the ring of the overhead bell to signal the door opening
and closing, followed by the polite chatter of the waitress
swapping pleasantries with another customer. But I didn't look.
I was too busy wondering whether the Italian police were going
to recognise him. I was a mere handful of words into Tom's
exchange with the officer when–

'I'm sorry, is this seat taken?'

There was a man standing in front of me, a lone diner who
had an embarrassingly incorrect reading of this situation. If I
had to put a number on it, I would have placed him in his early

forties: the beginnings of grey hair in the sideburns; deep laughter lines when he smiled at my confused expression. He was well over six feet tall, wearing jeans that looked close to tearing at the knees and a shirt that was speckled with magnolia paint.

I used my book to gesture to the barren landscape of the seating area. 'No, but none of those seats seem to be taken either.' Then I lowered my book, lowered my gaze and–

'One seafood combo.'

Fucking hell. I'd never been less pleased to see a medley of cod, haddock, crab and prawns set down in front of me. 'Thanks, that's great, thank you.'

'Did you decide where you're sitting yet, sir?' she asked the man who lingered.

He laughed and in my peripherals, I saw him rub at the back of his neck. 'Well, apparently not here.' He pointed to the table for two alongside my own. 'I'll just grab that table, if that's cool,' he paused for her to murmur in agreement, 'I'll take a Diet Coke while I'm thinking on food, too, please.'

'Sure thing.'

The sound of him pulling out his chair echoed through the space. I tried to wedge the book open in front of me, using my phone as a weight to keep the pages parted while I cut into the cod and paired it with a slice of boiled potato and cheese sauce.

'I'm new to the neighbourhood,' he said when the fork was seconds away from my mouth. 'I was just... being neighbourly,' he finished with an awkward laugh.

'Welcome to the neighbourhood.' I tucked the food in quickly before his response.

'Is it always this quiet here?'

I replied with a mouthful. 'On a Thursday.'

'What's so special about Thursdays?'

I sighed. All I wanted was to chew without speaking, while

simultaneously not having to wait for this conversation to be over before I could eat my food. *Sweet Lord, is that so much to ask?* 'There's a quiz on down the road; everyone flocks there on a Thursday.'

'But not you?'

'Not me.' I managed another bite.

'You sit here and read... What is it you're reading?'

'Patricia Highsmith.'

'Ah, Ripley?'

He won himself a point. I finished chewing a prawn before I answered. 'You're familiar with it.'

'Sort of,' he laughed nervously again, 'I'm familiar with the series.'

He lost a point. 'The books are better.'

'Aren't they always?'

The waitress reappeared then and I could have tipped her for distracting him. I managed three hungry mouthfuls with the enthusiasm of a woman who hasn't eaten in days, and I tried to remember when I last had actually eaten before this. I read three more pages and ate half of my cod fillet in the time it took for him to order fish and fries, which was a combination of words that I bitterly hated.

'Have you seen the series then?'

Another sigh tumbled out of me and I wondered whether there was any way at all to politely ask him to stop speaking. It wasn't something I'd ever found a means of saying to someone, but I knew there must be a trick to it; there had to be.

'No, only the books.'

'It's never clear to me how he gets away with so many murders.'

'Well,' I stabbed at a prawn with purpose, 'I've got five books to find out.'

He laughed and this time it was an easier sound. 'I'm Dean, by the way.'

'Caroline.'

'You're not from round here?'

I murmured in answer. *Clever boy*, I wanted to say with a pat on the head.

'You haven't stolen someone's identity to commit a few murders, have you?'

I turned and looked at Dean straight on then. He was smiling, crows' feet pinching at the sides of his eyes, and I wondered whether this classed as flirting for him, or whether he really was just being polite. 'It's hard to say, Dean. I haven't stolen someone's identity.' I turned back to my meal then; scored my way through a boiled potato, and dipped it against a pocket of sauce that had gathered in the curve of my plate. 'But I'm not quite sure I've felt myself lately, either.'

THE CRIME AT THE HOTEL CHRILLON
EPISODE 1

Release date: May 2015

Julie: Hello and welcome to a sparkly new podcast! This is *The Crime at the Hotel Chrillon* and, you probably guessed it, we're here to talk all about the crime at the Hotel Chrillon. Which I sort of feel like needs no introduction at this point, but we'll give it one all the same. I'm co-host of the show, Julie Cline, and I'll be joined each week by...

Sally: Sally Ruben! Hi, everyone. You might recognise us from our YouTube channel, *Dine, Wine and Crime,* but rather than wining and dining ourselves and settling down with a true crime documentary, on this show we're going to be bringing you live updates and commentary on the Hotel Chrillon case.

Julie: But we'll start with a little bit of backstory, to get everyone up to speed, and we figured the best starting point for this whole thing is Caroline Geel. The name on everyone's lips at the moment, don't you think?

Sally: [Nervous noise] I don't know, I feel like the name Noah Prescott is lingering on a few mouths, too, at the minute.

Julie: Of course, how could it not? Maybe we should start there, what do you think? [Pause, the sound of shuffling papers] Okay, so Noah is from Maine, USA, born and bred, he's a handyman, fond friend to many, and a doting father–

Sally: Ah, doting? Can we ring the alarm on that for a hot second? I've read reports that seem to suggest he never even disclosed to Caroline that he had a child.

Julie: But we haven't got confirmation on that, have we? Or have we?

Sally: Not yet, but there's new information coming *all* the time on this one, so it's probably only a matter of another news report before we hear more about the father of one.

Julie: *Alleged* father of one.

Sally: [Audible sigh] Alleged, fine, whatever. But these factoids don't just appear out of thin air, do they?

Julie: I don't know, Sal, with a case like this one? It's hard to tell the truth from the lies straight outta the gate.

TEA AND TRUE CRIME
EPISODE 502

Release date: May 2015

Lucy: Okay, folks, we're here with our strong cups of tea. Patrick?

Patrick: Here!

Lucy: And we're ready to spice up the podcast for you this week. Now, we know we usually focus on true crime that's based *in* the UK, but we're hoping that you'll allow us to make an exception.

Patrick: So we're going to hop across the pond for this week's episode and talk about... Caroline Geel!

Lucy: Who is a UK native, so we're only bending the rules a *tiny* bit.

Patrick: Sweet Jesus, who cares about bending the rules? This case is golden and it's blowing up mediascapes the whole world over. Caroline Geel, schoolteacher, journalist and two-time failed wife–

Lucy: Fuck off, that is not how we're introducing her. That's a toe away from victim-blaming.

Patrick: Harsh but fair. Right, I have a statement here from her first husband, Peter Borne, another UK native, that reads, *and I quote,* "Caroline was never the wifely type".

Lucy: I have the same sheet of paper in front of me right here, Paddy, so do you want to go ahead and read the rest of that statement?

Patrick: [Pause] I think I've done it justice.

Lucy: Okay, I'm going to go ahead and read the rest of that statement. "... never the wifely type, because she spent so much time trying to *shape a career for herself,* and even though I'd always thought we were heading towards starting a family, *she never expressed a desire for children."* My emphases there, listeners, forgive me. But are these the makings of a failed wife?

Patrick: Will you forgive me for ramping up the tension a smidge? We were at a nine, I was shooting for an eleven.

CRIME AND CULTURE
EPISODE 145

Release date: May 2015

Aiden: Good evening, everyone, and thanks for tuning in to this Friday's episode. I've got a lot of material to get through and half an hour to do it, so I'm going to jump right in and kick off the conversation with gun crime, America, and policing weapons. It probably won't surprise you to learn that we're also going to talk about Maine as part of this conversation, and the fact that Maine is a permitless carry state. Now, for those of you who don't know, that essentially means that you're allowed to carry a concealed firearm. There are a few more nuts and bolts to consider alongside that, but that's basically the way it goes down. The reason for that? Well, historically, Maine has been a state with ridiculously low gun crime rates, especially in comparison to the rest of the country. It still is, right, one crime alone can't change that. However, and that however is doing some heavy-lifting right here, one crime alone *can* make people wonder whether a permitless carry approach is the best way to go for *any* state – especially when a state that's enforcing that policy goes ahead and sees a crime take place, with a gun, in a hotel full of people at the time. There was no warning, there was no sign that this was about to happen, short of one person pulling a gun on another and the whole room ducking for cover, because of course that's what you'd do when someone, anyone, in any space, decides to open fire...

CHAPTER EIGHT

MAY 2015

I have a vivid memory of my mother putting my hair in overnight curling rags when I was a girl. She weaved them into my hair and then tucked them up in tight bunches. There was a talent show at school the next day, and I'd told her I wanted to look my best. I can remember the morning of the show, then, when one by one she unpinned the rags and let my hair tumble around my shoulders in fairytale corkscrew curls, and suddenly it didn't matter what I was doing or whether I would get a medal or even whether people would like what I planned to do. I remember thinking that above anything else, I was going to be the prettiest girl in school that day, and I was going to be the envy of every other girl – I felt certain of that much – which was all that seemed to matter at the time. And that's the memory that came back to me on one particular Friday afternoon when I was getting ready to meet Noah. I was using a curling iron and everything about it felt that bit less glamorous than when Mum had fashioned my corkscrews for me. But still, with a flourish, I unleashed another clump of hair from the clench of the hot iron and I watched it tumble loose around my shoulders, and I wondered whether I would be the prettiest woman in the bar of the Hotel Chrillon.

It seemed unlikely. I'd long lost the confidence to believe I might be the prettiest woman anywhere, at any time. But there was still a quiet joy in seeing my hair come together in loose waves here and tight curls there where the layers were shorter and easier to manipulate. It was no longer the bright and brilliant ginger of my childhood, but a dark auburn now, dulled by years of using products and failed attempts at dying it. Still, the curls and the colour combined gave me a look that was that bit more special than the average day, where it was normally tucked messily into a high bun and held out of the way of my face. I let loose the final bunch of hair and then sprayed three-strength hairspray in a mist around my head to fix everything in place. After that, I started with make-up. I opted for a concealer that was thin enough to let my natural freckles show, paired with a mascara that gave me a wide-eyed look that had nothing natural about it, but I thought the two might balance each other out. I painted on a deep red smear to my lips, paying close attention to the outline of my cupid's bow, making sure not to smudge the edges.

The last thing I did to ready myself for my afternoon date was to put on a pair of my mother's earrings – silver hoops that I'd begged from her when I was twenty-one and I'd hardly worn since – and a silver bracelet that I thought Peter might have given me. Or maybe it was Joel? I tried to remember as I struggled to shut the clasp. After that I piled everything into my handbag: lipstick, mobile and metal all knocking together as I pulled the lips closed. I slipped a thin beige overcoat round my shoulders to protect me from the chill that I thought would come later, and then I admired the look as a whole in the long-length mirror in my bedroom. I was wearing a red dress that I thought paired well with the lipstick; it was knee-length but with a flamenco dancer's dream hem, all loose ruffles and drama as I moved. I twisted from side to side and watched the dress kick around me, and I wondered whether it would photograph well.

The Hotel Chrillon was slightly more upmarket than anywhere Noah and I might usually meet on a Friday afternoon or evening for drinks. It wasn't uncommon for us to share a cocktail or two to mark the roll-in of a weekend, but it would usually be at a bar – or sometimes even at my place, with Noah arriving after work, kitted out with passion fruits and vodka. But I'd texted him at the start of the week to ask if we could try somewhere new and he'd replied with too much enthusiasm, so we were committed to this plan now. If he'd said no, if he'd said, that isn't the kind of place we go to, things might have worked out differently. As it was, I'd told him to wear something smart and when he replied to ask, like what, I'd suggested a white shirt, a fresh pair of jeans. "Something light."

On my walk there, Noah texted me to say the place seemed busy, so he was going in to get a table. I didn't reply. Instead, I only listened to the quiet of the landscape coming to a grinding halt in readiness for the weekend: cars idling in traffic; teenagers having been unleashed from the confines of their school enclosures. I walked past Teddy, who I imagined hadn't been in school at all. He did a double take when he saw me, only registering who I was after a first look, and then he looked me up and down with a smirk as he walked by. My heel-clicks came to a halt at the steps leading into the hotel foyer, and I took a second to scrunch my hair up on one side then the other, to liven up my curls again from the damage done by the soft breeze on the way there. Once inside, I told the front of house – a young woman in a skirt-suit who looked deeply out of place in the clothing, not least because of the oversized ring in her nostril – that I was meeting someone in the bar, and she walked me through.

Noah was tucked away at the far end of the room, in a cluster of tables that were dressed for parties of two. He stood when he saw me walk in and I thought it might have been the most gentlemanly gesture he'd ever made. We're both making an effort, I thought with a sad smile as I crossed the room. He was wearing light blue jeans that didn't have rips in, or a work stain in sight, and a white shirt – tucked in, to show the shine of a brown belt – crisp white, and so free of wrinkles, I thought it must have come straight from a shop dummy. When there were only two strides left between us, he held his arms wide and presented himself with a toothy smile. 'Smart enough?'

'Just right.'

Noah leaned forward to kiss my cheek and I heard him inhale deeply when he was close. A small shudder ran through him that I recognised as want; it was something he always did, like a tic to indicate sexual arousal. He moved back to his side of the table then, while I slipped my coat free from my shoulders and draped it over the back of my chair. I set my handbag on the floor at a reachable distance from my chair and smoothed down my wild dress before I sat.

'Caroline, you look... I mean, damn... That dress... Your hair...'

I laughed. 'You seem to be struggling to finish your sentences.'

'Well yeah,' he spluttered, 'have you seen you?' He leaned across the table to lessen the distance and spoke in a hushed tone. 'Are you sure you even want to be here right now? I mean, we could head straight back to yours, get cocktails to go or something? What d'you say? I'll put that dress to good use.'

It was when he spoke like this that I wondered what had

drawn me to Noah in the first place. Sometimes he opened his mouth and out came the boys I wanted attention from when I was ten years younger. Of course I was settled with Peter by then, and the idea of infidelity had never appealed much, but I'd never been blind to the fact that while both of us could have been, *should* have been, sowing our proverbial oats, we'd been hunkered down in each other's study halls instead, cramming for the next exam or planning out our life together. Noah might have been a latent expression of teenage decision-making on my part back then. The type of man who I would have searched for in the Student Union bar, locked eyes with across the room, blushed at the sight of, only to squeeze Peter's hand that bit tighter before agreeing that yes, it was busy, and yes, of course, we could leave.

'Sorry to intrude...' A young waiter came to a stop at the side of our table. He was neatly turned out, hair properly parted and pasted down with hair gel that he would regret when he was my age. He was wearing a pant-waistcoat combination with a white shirt beneath it. I was sure that everything had the hotel's logo printed on it, even the trousers. He was wearing a name badge that said, "You can call me Ron."

'Will you folks be wanting to order any food today?'

I glanced over at Noah and let my eyes dip to his watch. We had time.

'Do you want anything to eat?' I asked him, smiling. It did something for his ego to be asked. He'd never said as much, of course, but the impact of it was observable in him. He sat a little straighter and glanced around the table, I assumed for a menu.

'We have bar snacks that are available, or I can see what the restaurant availabil–'

'No,' I snapped and both men turned to me. 'Sorry,' I forced a laugh, a girlish sound, 'I'd prefer to stay here rather than move to the restaurant, if that's okay with you?' I turned to Noah as though seeking his approval.

'Is there a menu for the bar snacks?' Noah asked in a tone that suggested he thought it might be a stupid question. Of course, in somewhere like the Hotel Chrillon it wasn't. I knew Noah well enough to know that his expectation of bar snacks was a bag of peanuts and a packet of pretzels.

'There is,' Ron answered, 'I'll just go and get that for you. Can I get you any drinks while I'm at it?'

'I'll take an old-fashioned,' I answered, my smile tight.

Noah shot me a quizzical glance before turning to order. 'I'll take a beer.'

'I'll get those for you now.'

'An old-fashioned?'

I shrugged. 'I felt like something different.'

He gave me a look as though he were inspecting me for something. His eyes narrowed to slits and he tilted his head to one side, then the other. 'Have you been writing today?'

'You make it sound like I've been at home shooting up.'

Noah laughed. 'Sometimes that's what you're like, when you're on it.'

'I don't know what you mean,' I fidgeted with the edge of a napkin, 'but yes, I've been writing today, thank you for asking.'

'The novel?'

I noticed he asked without using his usual mocking intonation, and it made me warm to him for a second. My shoulders relaxed slightly, and I felt my thighs press harder against the chair, as though I were experiencing something like a full body exhale.

'On the new novel, yes.'

'How's it going?'

I matched his earlier expression: narrowed eyes, inspecting. 'Why are you asking?'

Noah laughed and rubbed at the back of his neck. He reached across the table with an open palm and I realised he expected me to take his hand, so I did. His working man's thumb rubbed at the smooth skin of my wrist. 'Because it's important to you. You care about this stuff, so I want to try to start caring about this stuff.'

'Noah, that's...'

'One old-fashioned?' I broke contact with Noah and leaned back to clear Ron's route to the table. 'One beer, and one menu. I'll give you folks a minute to have a browse through.'

'Thanks, bud,' Noah answered, snatching the menu before I could. He would look at the prices first, I knew, and although he didn't say anything, I watched as his eyes shifted and widened, then widened again as he moved to the second column of options. 'These are some... interesting bar snacks,' he laughed, 'here, you decide.'

I studied one side then the other: popcorn with sesame-glazed pistachios; German soft pretzel sticks; queso fundido; jalapeño-lime pepitas; fig and prosciutto flatbreads. I wanted to order one of everything, lay the table out for a feast and let him sample the texture, colour, taste of it all. It felt like an exercise in enlightenment.

'How about... fried oysters with remoulade?' I looked up at him and he shrugged. 'We could also get some butternut squash and sage wontons to try, they sound interesting, and I'm sort of taken with the idea of the Bloody Mary-pickled green beans. That sounds like it could be a fun thing to try,' I looked up again, 'don't you think?'

Noah laughed in nervous answer and fidgeted with the front of his hair. He had a cowlick that he was deeply self-conscious of – and he hated it when I called it that. But whenever he was unsure in a situation, that's where his hand wandered to. 'Honestly, it all sounds fantastic, so whatever you want is great with me.' He sipped his beer. 'Shall I try to get the waiter's attention?'

'There's no rush,' I answered as he started to look around. 'We have time, right?'

'Right.' He eased the menu free from my hand and replaced it with the heat of his palm, resuming our contact. 'Before food, you were going to tell me about the book.'

I lowered my gaze. 'I don't know that I was.'

'Come on,' he yanked at me, 'just give me a rough idea of it.'

'Well, right now the thing is half-finished, printed and locked in my office safe. That's where the book is at.' I managed a laugh. 'But I'm just struggling with the plot of it right now, that's all. The characters are sound.'

'What are the characters like?'

I shrugged and sipped my drink to buy myself a second of time. 'She's a woman on a spiral.'

'Where's she spiralling to?'

'I'm not sure yet,' I admitted, and I was painfully aware of how sad I sounded.

'Maybe by the next time we visit this place, you'll know.' Noah's upbeat tone was over-compensating for the dull thrum of my own, I thought, and I gifted him an appreciative smile. 'Come on, I'm going to catch the waiter and order this food, then we can really get the weekend started, eh?'

While he was away from the table I leaned over to part the lips of my handbag; I wanted to check everything was in there that should be. It was a nervous tic of mine. I felt around for the tube of my lipstick and, with that in hand, I walked my fingertips around the space until I landed on something cool. I checked to see that Noah was still at the bar before I pulled it out, and then I quickly opened the mirror to check my mouth was in order. I didn't need the lipstick. The red outline was fixed in place just the same, despite the press of my glass having been against it, so I snapped the mirror closed and replaced it in my open bag. I pulled out a squat bottle of perfume and sprayed my neck first and then one wrist, before dropping that back into the bag, too, and dabbing my wrists together.

'All sorted,' Noah announced while I was still righting myself. I didn't have time to close my bag, but the next table was a good metre and then some away from us so I thought everything would be safe. 'Ron said it'll be out in a jiffy,' he parroted in a mocking tone, 'who would have thought people actually speak like that?'

I ignored the comment. 'Thanks for ordering the food.'

'It's okay,' he tucked his chair back in, 'I started a tab.'

I couldn't help but wonder who would be paying for it.

'Now I've told you about my writing, or lack of writing,' I forced a smile as though the admission didn't bother me, 'why don't you tell me about your day?'

'Are you for real?' He sipped his beer and wiped a foam bubble from the corner of his mouth. 'I spend my days doing gardening work and odd jobs. You *never* ask about my day.'

'Well I'm asking now. I'm taking an interest. You care about this stuff...'

Noah laughed. 'Okay, okay,' he held his hands up as though in a defensive stance, 'you *actually* care about the stuff you do for a living, it's *actually* important to you. The stuff I do for a living just keeps a roof over my head. It's a decent living, sure, but it's hardly rocket science. Today I spent the first half of the day mowing lawns around the neighbourhood and then this afternoon I trimmed back all the rose bushes that are growing around the Acre Farm. That's literally my day.' He laughed again, but the longer he'd wandered into his explanation the more hard-edged his voice had become. It was the longest time I'd ever heard him talk about his work.

'What did you want to do when you were a kid?' I asked

then, and the question clearly surprised him. 'I always wanted to be a writer,' I added, in the hope that if I made the first move then he may feel less nervous about shifting a pawn out of place, 'I always wanted to do that, and all the other stuff was only ever in support of that, really. What did you always want to do?'

He huffed a laugh and pulled his hand away from mine. I hadn't realised we were still making physical contact until it was snatched from me. Instead, Noah weighed his beer bottle in his hand and studied the label before taking a swig. 'Some of us don't need dreams, Caroline. Some of us are happy with our legacy being friends, maybe a kid or two, and a decent living. It doesn't always have to be about getting your name in lights, you know?'

I murmured in agreement before sipping my own drink. *Wrong*, I thought. *Wrong, wrong, wrong.*

Noah only picked at the food we ordered, but he managed another two beers against my Diet Coke. I decided that one old-fashioned was enough. I enjoyed drinking but I'd always struggled with being drunk; I thought it was likely a control thing, something about having my full wits about me. For anyone to see me blisteringly drunk they would need an evening with me at home, when I could lock myself in before my behaviour became too much of something in the outside world. That said, Noah eyed me with some suspicion when I refused the offer of a second cocktail; I mightn't get drunk on our evenings out together, but I could ordinarily run to two or three drinks without concern. That night was different though. I sipped at the dregs of my drink and focussed on the ice cubes knocking together. One of them bit against my upper lip as I tipped the glass back to drain the remnants and I worried for my lipstick. Meanwhile, Noah neared the bottom of his third beer. He wasn't drunk either though. Noah was a well-built man: well over six feet tall with bench press abilities that meant nothing to me, I only knew he was strong. He flicked at the label with the tip of his index finger, worrying at the softened paper, and I thought he was about to say something stupid like, "Will you marry me?", but instead he laughed and said nothing.

'Have you enjoyed this?' I asked. 'Coming somewhere different?'

He smiled. 'I'm about ready for a pizza,' he nodded at the remains of food on the table as he spoke, though he kept his tone light and playful with it, 'but yeah, it's been nice, it's been nice to talk and... I don't know, see you like this.'

'See me like this?'

'Mm,' he twirled the bottle three-sixty degrees, 'you seem different.'

'Bad different?

Noah shrugged. 'Just different.'

'Is there anything else I can get for you both?' Ron appeared then and busied himself with stacking half-empty small plates on top of each other.

'I think we'll be leaving soon,' I directed the comment more to Noah, an implied question to make him feel involved, 'but thank you.'

'We'll take the bill, buddy, if that's okay,' Noah added.

'I'll be right back with that.'

I didn't like time-pressured decision-making. But there's something to be said for having your hand forced in a situation. I reached across the table to give Noah's hand a squeeze and we swapped a look that the drinkers around us might have described as soft. I wondered how we were being, how we had been perceived. Did we look strange together, or was there something just right about the woman out for drinks with a man very clearly younger than herself? It was only ten years, but it was observable, and I'd always wondered what people had to say about that when I wasn't listening.

I smiled, squeezed, and then let go of Noah's hand, and that's when I reached down to my handbag. I pulled out the Beretta Tomcat – Joel had let me choose for myself and I think I'd been drawn to it for the name alone – and I think I saw Noah frown when I extended my arm out towards him. I'm not sure, but he might have frowned.

And then I emptied the chamber into his chest.

TEA AND TRUE CRIME
EPISODE 502

Release date: May 2015

Lucy: But can we take a hot five to talk about the fact that she shot her boyfriend with a gun that her husband bought for her?

Patrick: What do you get for the woman who has everything? [Laughter]

Lucy: Pat, I'm serious! Doesn't that make it even more... icky? I don't know, I don't even know what word I want to use right there, but Jesus, hello. Who takes someone shopping for a *gun*? Is that a normal thing to do?

Patrick: It's a culture thing though, right? Joel – Joel, am I getting that name right?

Lucy: Mhmm.

Patrick: Joel has already gone on record to say that he was concerned about her being safe and protected. He had a gun, albeit one that was in storage still from before he moved over for work or whatever, so I guess it was already a *normal* thing, as far as he was concerned, for people to own guns.

Lucy: So, she *had* to have a gun just because she was in America? I don't buy that.

Patrick: Well, sure, she didn't *have* to have a gun, but she did. But do you know something else?

Lucy: What?

Patrick: She didn't *have* to shoot the man in the chest until the pistol rang empty, either.

THE MAINE MURDER MYSTERY CHANNEL
EPISODE 238

Release date: May 2015

Billy: Jesus H Christ, though, can you *imagine* being Ron in that situation? The poor guy serves them food and drinks all night, jokes with them, generally acts like a good host for the hotel and *this* is how he gets tipped.

Liv: Ron was... [Pause] I wanted to fact check this before I said it, Ron was actually hospitalised with shock after the shooting happened. By all accounts he was a hot mess, shaking, the works.

Billy: But wouldn't you be? Like, have *you* ever seen someone shot before?

Liv: Only in shamefully grainy CCTV footage.

Billy: Exactly. Imagine being one of the poor assholes with a front row seat to that.

CHAPTER NINE

The good thing about being a writer was that it gave me years of arduous practise at not speaking to anyone for long periods of time, bar myself. Perhaps that's why, after the panic and the police and the handcuffs, I managed to go a whole day having only said two words. They were holding me in a local station until my lawyer arrived, which looked to be taking some time – longer than I'd hoped, anyway. I was assured that they'd called him for me, after I'd declined to use my phone call myself. The man was a high-flyer based in New York now, but I'd gathered from his website that he was from Maine originally, and although I knew I was taking something of a chance – and expecting him to undergo one hell of a commute – I wagered there wasn't a power-hungry suit in the land who could resist the temptation of a high-profile case involving a woman who'd just shot her lover in a well-populated hotel bar. Especially when that woman had only said two words since her arrest.

Lucas Williams had a reputation for taking media circus cases. From what I'd seen in videos online, he looked to be a believer in the old adage that there was no such thing as bad publicity; even if that involved representing a murderer in court, which I was fairly certain he'd done at least once, and that made my own circumstances seem nearly unremarkable. The last case he was known for taking, dragging, kicking and howling through the American judicial system, was for a man who had allegedly shot his wife whilst he was sleepwalking. Williams bargained like a British grandmother at a car boot sale and the killer in question served eighteen months. I'd watched so many videos of the lawyer being interviewed that I felt as though I already knew him – which was why I was willing to bet his retainer fee that he would take my case, providing I could get him back into the state and comfortably settled in a seat opposite me. It would be a challenge, the whole trial would be a challenge, but Williams struck me as the sort of character who would welcome that. And if he did, then he'd find his retainer weighed out in $100 notes in my office safe at home.

'Geel.' The guard made his entrance known with a firm kick against the metal of the door as he entered the cell space. 'Think you'll grace us with some good conversation today?'

I smiled and shook my head.

'You're gonna be a pain in the ass, lady, I can tell that much. Here,' he put down a plastic bowl that I peered inside, and a beaker of water, too, 'keep your strength up. I'm not having anyone accuse us of not having fed you right while you're here.'

On a scale of one to hungry, I'd been unfathomably ravenous since Noah. I waited for the guard – Officer Kennedy, one of the men who'd arrested me – to slam the cell door behind him because otherwise it felt too much like shame eating, to be watched while I shovelled oats and milk into my mouth with my plastic spoon. When I knew he was gone, I tucked great mouthfuls between my lips, loading the next one before the previous one was hardly even swallowed. I choked on the clog of the mixture and coughed, loud and hard to clear the obstruction, before I started eating again. And before I knew it, everything was gone. I grabbed at the beaker and chugged water down as though I hadn't known fluids for days, and when the cup was empty I set it, and my bowl, on the floor to be collected. I lay flat on my back then and placed my hands on my stomach, and I imagined the water and oats and milk meeting in my belly. The longer I imagined it, the bigger the bloat felt.

After breakfast I slept for two hours, only waking at the sound of the door opening again, and through slits I peered at the new arrival. I hadn't met this officer yet.

'Up you get, Geel, lawyer's here.'

I opened my mouth to speak but then I remembered I didn't do that anymore. Instead, I only nodded and stood, and I kept my excitement sealed behind locked lips. But on the walk from my cell to the meeting room, I fizzed with enthusiasm.

So imagine my disappointment when I rounded the corner and saw a squat, bald man with bottle-top glasses and a sweaty gleam on his forehead. I turned to the guard who'd brought me here and shook my head.

'Look, I know this isn't the guy you asked us to call, but he obviously isn't coming, and we can't hold you here forever. Talk to this guy, tell him your story. Helluva story,' he held the door open for me and I almost expected him to tap my rear in encouragement, 'I'm sure he'd love to hear all about it.'

'Miss Geel.' I hovered on the boundary of the room, fidgeted with my cuffed hands. 'I'm Alistair James.'

Never trust a first-name-last-name. I smiled at the memory of Mum telling me that, even though I couldn't remember the context. Not for the first time then, I wondered how she must be handling all of this – whether she was.

'Adams!'

A shout came from down the corridor and the officer who had brought me here – Officer Adams, apparently – turned to greet his colleague: another man who I didn't recognise. I wondered how many officers one small-town police station could possibly need. Really, how much crime was there to fight? *Oh.* I smiled, nearly laughed, but I let the reaction settle.

The other guard whispered something to Adams, who huffed a laugh in answer. 'It's your lucky day, Geel.'

'Sorry, Mr James, it looks like you've had a wasted journey,' Unknown Officer started to explain.

Adams led me by the arm, away from the open doorway and further down the corridor we'd started on. He didn't say a word, and I wanted to ask, but I couldn't bring myself to. After a small stretch of walking – the most exercise I'd had in days and I was dismayed to feel how much my legs ached – we arrived at another room, another door. Behind this one, there was a man wearing a suit that looked as though it would cover my mortgage payment for a month if not longer. It was black, with a slim pinstripe running through it. He'd paired it with a white shirt, a black tie, and a pensive expression that I knew photographed well. In another life, Lucas Williams looked like the sort of man my mother might have hoped I would bring home – maybe sometime after the first divorce, but before the second marriage.

'Miss Geel,' he said when I took nervous steps into the room, 'thank you, officer, we'll be fine from here.'

'Give us a knock if you need anything,' Adams said as he closed the door.

Williams flashed me a tight smile and gestured to the seat opposite his own. There was a fresh yellow legal pad in front of him, on the table between us, and I couldn't help but think of the times I'd watched this exchange play out in televised dramas. He waited until I was sitting before he took his own seat, and then he smoothed down his tie, cleared his throat and stared at me. 'Do you want to tell me why I'm here?'

'I shot my...' I didn't know what Noah had been. *Boyfriend* was infantile, *lover* was too French. 'I shot someone.'

'Shot someone dead, from what I hear.'

'Mhmm,' I quietly agreed, 'in a hotel bar.'

'He cheat on you?'

I narrowed my eyes at the question. 'It wasn't that sort of relationship.'

'Was he abusive?'

'No.'

'Did you want to marry him?'

My squint tightened further. 'No.'

'Was there money involved?'

'No.'

'I'm running out of motives, Miss Geel. Do you wanna tell me why you shot him?'

'No.'

Williams cleared his throat and smiled. 'So why am I here?'

'I want to get away with murder.'

'And you think I'm the man to help you do that?'

'If you're at all worth your fee.'

'And you can afford my fee?'

'It's in my safe at home. You'll need access to my personal effects. The key is in the inside pocket of the handbag that I had on me when I was brought in.'

'That'd be the handbag you pulled the gun out from, am I right?'

I nodded. 'That one, yes.'

'Well, all right then.' He reached into a hidden pocket of his suit and pulled out a pen. He clicked the tip of it with purpose and sat poised with the nib hovering over an empty sheet of paper. 'Do you need anything before we start? Water?'

'I need a favour.'

He laughed. 'Miss Geel, I'm *already* doing you a favour.' But he jerked his chin towards me, as though encouraging my request out.

'Underneath your fee, in the safe, there's a manuscript...'

CHAPTER TEN

Lucas – he'd told me to call him Lucas, and I'd extended the courtesy of telling him to call me Caroline – had earned his fee twice over by the time we were through arraignment. He and I had next to no time to get acquainted while he explained the proceedings and told me I'd need to attend, but that I wouldn't necessarily need to speak – apart from entering my plea.

'And that's when you say "not guilty" and I take it from there.'

'I'm sorry?'

Funnily enough, the judge overseeing the proceedings had a similar reaction to my own on hearing that plea. She – because of course, deliberately perhaps, it was a female judge – looked as though she'd misheard me, then she went ahead and detailed everything she already knew about the case, as though I hadn't been there when the events unfolded, then she asked me to repeat the plea. She gave me the space to speak for a second time, asking me if I was sure that the plea I was entering was what I'd meant to say. Lucas answered for me – 'Miss Geel pleads not guilty, Your Honour.' – which under normal circumstances was something I would have hated, him having spoken for me. But in speaking those words aloud to her, I'd already hit my quota for speaking to people besides Lucas for the day, and I hadn't been in a mind to say it again. I was finding it increasingly difficult to speak to anyone who wasn't Lucas by then, though I wasn't altogether sure why. It felt as though I'd taken a vow of silence without knowing it, only to be reminded when I opened my mouth and nothing but hot air rushed out of me. I'd even wondered whether it was a self-defence valve that had been opened since, but again I couldn't be sure. I wasn't expert enough.

While the judge digested this information, looking every bit like Noah had when he first saw the food menu at the Hotel Chrillon, the district attorney only snorted.

'Your Honour, can you kindly request that the DA drop his attitude?'

'Your Honour, can you kindly remind Mr Williams that his client shot a man at point blank range, thereby murdering him in front of a room full of people?' The DA looked at a sheet of paper as he spoke, miming the act of reading aloud. He was three inches shorter than Lucas and you could tell by how he carried himself that he wasn't happy about that. He stuck his chest out, every bit the peacock, and when he'd finished speaking he still didn't look at the judge, nor at Lucas, but directly at me. If a man in a bar had looked at me like that, it would have been expression enough to make me leave early and walk home with my keys wedged between my knuckles. In this setting, I wasn't sure how to react; I thought reaching into Lucas's suitcase to find his house keys probably wouldn't be appropriate, for so many reasons – not least because now, I had form.

'Mr Williams, I assume you have a plan for how you'll be defending your client?' the judge asked as though neither man had spoken, and I warmed to her. She was a woman twenty years my senior with a brilliantly severe grey bob that must have had her at the hairdressers every two weeks to have the points sharpened. She was wearing catlike glasses, flicked up at the corner on each side, and a lick of light brown lipstick that was enough to define her lips but not so deep a shade that people wouldn't take her seriously. Her entire appearance spoke to her ongoing battle to demonstrate her authority. She was a character so good that I wished I'd written her before meeting her, just so I could take original credit.

'I'll be arranging a series of interviews and evaluations for my client, Your Honour, and I also need time to speak to various witnesses.'

'The witnesses that saw her shoot the man?' the DA injected.

'Noah,' Lucas answered, 'if we can do him the respect of calling him by his name.'

'You've got some nerve, walking into this state and–'

'That'll be all, from both of you,' she cut across their sparring. '*Both* of you will need time to liaise with witnesses,' she said pointedly, directing the comment more to the DA than Lucas, which seemed to make the former recoil and the latter quite smug with himself, 'and I think you're wise, Mr Williams, to be arranging for those assessments. There's more to this than meets the eye. ' I'd dropped my eyes to my lap by then, where I was watching my hands knot together, their skin already broken from days away from my usual skincare regime. I wondered how the rest of me must look. 'Isn't there, Miss Geel?'

My head shot up at the question. I could tell she didn't expect me to answer, but something passed between us during that moment all the same – an unspoken conversation. There followed background chatter of bail and trials, and other things that I didn't have an interest in. I was happy to let them unfold their official words without me hearing them. Somehow, it didn't seem important anymore.

'Miss Geel will need to be moved to the nearest available jail, at the State's earliest convenience, but given the high profile nature of this case already, we'll endeavour to make sure the location is an appropriate one, rather than a hothouse for the media. Is there anything else, either of you?' She glanced between the beasts. Lucas shook his head and the DA shrugged, a petulant child who hadn't quite got his way. 'That'll be all for now.'

'Are you hungry?' Lucas asked me in a low voice as he leaned over to collect his things. 'It's way past my lunchtime and I'm dying for a burger.'

I don't know how he did it. But by the time we were back at the police station, there was an interview room waiting for us that stank rich of fries and charred meat when we walked in. Officer Adams rolled his eyes at me when we walked past him and into the room, but I couldn't understand what the gesture meant. Lucas smoothed down his tie before he sat at the table and he made a soft clucking noise at the smell of the food, inhaling so deeply that I was surprised the contents of the table didn't move an inch towards him. He gestured for me to take my seat, too, which I did, and I rested my hands in a bunching on the table.

'Please be kind enough to remove Miss Geel's cuffs before you leave, Officer...'

'Adams.' He closed the distance between us. I was sure he'd already been halfway to leaving. 'And sure.' He didn't roll his eyes at me this time, but he did flash another expression at me – contempt, maybe, and I wondered whether men would always give me these looks now: judgement; suspicion; disapproval.

Though I wondered, too, how exactly that was any different to before.

'You have a lot of clout in every room you enter,' I said when we were alone again.

Lucas laughed and tucked a fry into his mouth. 'I wouldn't say that.'

'The judge got along well enough with you.'

'The judge is a fair woman. She and I have worked together before.'

'You've tried a case in Maine before?'

He laughed. 'I've tried cases everywhere. Eat your food,' he nodded towards the brown bag that was sitting squat in front of me, 'I won't be able to pull these strings for every visit so you should make the most of it.'

'If I'd known it was a special occasion,' I answered as I unfolded the lips of the paper, 'I would have asked for cigarettes instead of food.'

Lucas mumbled something that I didn't hear as he wiped his hands on a nearby napkin. Then he ferreted around the inside pocket of his suit – another pinstripe, this time in grey – and dropped a packet of Marlboros on the table between us. 'Why have one when you can have both?' I reached for the box, but he paused my hand by placing his own on top of it. 'When you've eaten.'

There was something paternal in the gesture. Again, it was something I might have hated under other circumstances, but somehow Lucas looked to be an exception to my rules when it came to other people dictating my behaviours. So I answered by pulling my hand back to the bag in front of me. My fingers crushed up against the burger that was inside and I yanked it out. Thick bread, thick meat, with a medley of lettuce and red sauce sneaking out of the sides. I licked the edge of the bun clean and felt the ketchup burn at the back of my throat. It was the first thing I'd eaten in days that wasn't beige.

'Strawberry or chocolate?' he asked as he peered over the lids of the drinks.

'Strawberry.'

He pushed one towards me, followed by a straw. I was too busy inhaling my burger to answer him with anything more substantial than a noise.

CHAPTER ELEVEN

The move to a jail didn't prove to be an easy thing. I had expected to be thrown into the back of a van with blacked out windows and carted to the nearest slum before the day in court was out. But after the arraignment nothing much seemed to happen. Two days passed before Officer Kennedy explained that they couldn't find a secure space for me elsewhere yet, which meant they were stuck with me here. They weren't his exact words, though I do distinctly remember his use of the word "secure" – as though there were many less secure spaces just waiting for me, if only they weren't bound by duty to ensure that didn't happen. He coupled his announcement with a lunchtime drink and sandwich – ham and mustard on white bread, an apple and a beaker of water – that he left behind, with strict instructions that I was to eat everything. Having gone on strike from speaking, the guards whose job it was to take care of me, in a fashion at least, seemed worried that food might be the next thing for me to sacrifice. It wouldn't be, though. I was still nursing the fierce hunger that had come with killing a man.

I thought two hours must have passed by the time I saw

another guard. This time, a woman, the first I'd seen working here since this circus had started. She lingered at the doorway looking in at me, making me feel every bit the caged animal. A moment or two passed before she unlocked the door to my cell and studied the empty lunch tray that I'd left on the floor.

'You managed to eat then,' she said as she leaned over to collect it. She was a stout woman, though I thought the light brown uniform likely wasn't doing her any favours. She had matching brown hair that was folded into a tight bun at the back of her head, and I struggled to imagine her in her daily life, appearing anything but brown, brown, brown.

It was a game that I'd started to play with myself: imagining the guards outside. Kennedy, I had decided, definitely had a wife at home and probably two children. Everything about him seemed nuclear. Adams was too young still to have made that sacrifice yet, but I thought he probably had a girlfriend; he was too conventionally attractive not to have at least one, but I couldn't decide whether he was immoral enough to have more than that. I imagined them in their jeans and khaki trousers, patterned shirts with slicked back hair; wide smiles and nudged shoulders as they cosied up to their drinking buddies and said things like, 'That Geel woman, she's a piece of work...' Though maybe I was being hard on them. After all, I hadn't really given them, personally, any reason to say a bad word about me.

'The boys tell me you aren't much of a talker.' I flashed her a thin smile and shook my head. 'That's a shame because I'm a real listener, you know?' She leaned up against the open doorway, the tray balanced in front of her. 'I wondered whether there was anything you wanted to talk about while it's just us? Anything you might want to tell me about... I don't know... Noah Prescott, for example?'

I narrowed my eyes. Is this a police interview? I wondered as I pulled my legs up beneath me on the cot bed, making myself smaller still, pressing my back against the cold brick of the wall to push myself as far away from the woman as the room would allow.

'There's no pressure to, Caroline. I just wanted you to know that there's someone here for you. We aren't all against you.' She laughed then. 'Well, some of us are. But some of us aren't. If you change your mind, you just give me a holler, okay? Or give me a knock,' she tapped at the door with a knuckle then, as though I mightn't have understood her meaning, 'and I'll come trotting down here for a chat. Otherwise,' she checked her watch, 'I'll see you in a couple of hours for dinner.' She shut the door but spoke through the small open hatch of it to add, 'I can't promise it'll be burgers this time, though.'

I couldn't decide whether it was a dig or a sincere comment, but either way I let it hang dead between us. I tipped my head back and closed my eyes while she looked in on me still. I don't know how long she stayed there before finally admitting defeat and going to mind whatever other criminals she was hoping to bond with. Honestly though, I thought as I settled into a more comfortable position and listened to the whir and glug of my digestion, she wants to bond with me? The woman didn't even tell me her name.

There wasn't much to do apart from re-live it all. In the days of waiting for Lucus there was so much time and space to think in – not literally, of course, given that I'd been relegated to what was by any other name a box room. It reminded me too much of my first bedroom as a child, with a single bed wedged up into the corner to maximise the space. Though there was a distinct lack of teddy bears, tacked up posters, and pink things. I wasn't sure I'd appreciate them if I were given the opportunity to install them here, though. The blank walls at least gave me a page to imagine – not least given that my request for a State-approved yellow legal pad and a pen hadn't been granted yet. I wasn't sure whether it would be, given the many ways a woman might kill herself with those two articles alone. Not that I would. Even in my current state, with my hair a mess of grease and rat's tails and my skin a winter grey, I thought far too highly of myself to end it all now.

I lay back on the cot and felt the knots of my spine press into the slim mattress, and I stared at the blank pages around me, and I remembered. Noah had seen the gun, I thought. It's a cliché but in situations such as these everything really does happen so fast. But I was sure I could remember a narrowing and widening of the eyes, as though I were observing a snap realisation happening. Did he lift his hands to protect himself? I couldn't remember that detail, no matter how times I asked it of myself. But I *did* remember the pressure of the first shot, how it felt as though my entire body had been catapulted backwards into my seat; which is how Noah had looked, too, after the first one. There was a scream after that, and by then the shots were coming thick and fast and easy. I emptied the chamber, because I remember pressing the trigger over and again until there was nothing but an empty click. I'm sure people around me must have been screaming, louder, more of them, but I couldn't hear a thing. *Was that because of the gunshots?*

There was a long time after the gun was emptied when no one seemed to be doing anything at all, although I knew that couldn't possibly be true, not really. That's how it seemed though. Like for as long as a minute or two, I only sat opposite Noah's awkwardly slumped body and watched as his shirt slowly coloured. It was a creeping pattern, the way red wine moves across thick cream carpet when it isn't dabbed at quickly enough. Or the way blood moves through water when you cut yourself shaving in the bathtub. Or the way black coffee comes to take up more and more of a white bedsheet when you are enjoying the soft sunshine of a late morning with a lover.

I rested the gun on the table and I didn't think to pick it up again. I wondered whether it was in the same building as me now. I had walked through the madding crowds around me, through the foyer of the hotel where the front desk was now empty, bodies having scarpered into, underneath, pressed against any safe space they could find. There were four steps leading from the hotel to the pavement outside and I remember sitting on the second one, arranging my dress around me to ensure there was nothing indecent on display. Did I collect my coat before I left? The sun appeared from behind a cloud and I thought I could recall the soft warmth of it against my arms, so I mustn't have had my jacket. I closed my eyes and upturned my face how a content animal might. And I remembered waiting for them to come–

'Caroline?'

My eyes snapped open and my head turned towards the open doorway of my cell, where the unnamed female officer was standing. She wasn't holding a dinner tray, and I wondered what time that must make it.

'Look, I have to put these on,' she gestured with the handcuffs I hadn't realised she was holding, 'but if that's okay with you, then I thought we could take a turn around the gardens out back. It isn't much space, but it's more than in here, and you'd be entitled to exercise time if we'd... well, if we'd managed to move you. What do you say?' She cocked her head to one side as though she were talking to a child. 'It's sunny out there. I think it'll do you some good, just to have a turn around the world, see something other than these walls.'

I looked back at the wall ahead of me then, where the memory of Noah was written, and I watched as one by one the words disappeared; a finger on the backspace bar that didn't let up. I swung my legs down from the cot and held my wrists out towards her. She was right, though it made me uneasy to admit it. But I thought five minutes in the sunshine would likely do me some good.

CHAPTER TWELVE

Days rolled by without much happening at all. The male guards treated me with contempt and the female guard – Officer Clarence, as I had since learned she was called – looked to be spending more and more time caring for me, even though I still hadn't shared a word with her. She tried for conversation often, during every walk around the gardens, which we were having once a day – or at least, once a day when she was on shift. There had been an entire day when my only contact with another living body was Officer Kennedy bringing me my meals and, later, collecting the empty plates. It didn't escape my attention that he left me with the empty breakfast bowl until he brought my lunch, the empty lunch plate until he brought my dinner, limiting contact with me as best he could. Clarence was different, though; she seemed less timid than the men, and I wondered whether she thought she had less to worry about.

I drew the line at keeping a tally chart of days carved into the wall of my cell, though I'd be lying if I said it hadn't crossed my mind. Still, I think it was the sixth day when Lucas visited me again. I thought of him often during those days in between, and I spent too much time imagining what he might be doing and who he might be talking to; I worried what people might say, whether it would colour his view of me, which seemed a strange thing to give energy to. Nevertheless, the worry was there. And I found that when Adams came to unleash me from my cell with a curt nod and the announcement that Lucas was here, my relief was embarrassing. Thank God, I thought, he hasn't left me.

Lucas was wearing another suit: navy blue with a thicker pinstripe than the others, and it crossed my mind that perhaps this was his thing. In the same way my mother always wore hoop earrings, or Noah would only wear jeans that had rips in – apart from that one time he didn't.

'Caroline,' Lucas gestured to the seat opposite him, 'sorry it's been so long.' His tone was friendly, light, as though we were there for a mild-mannered catch-up with each other rather than a legal interview. He waited until Adams had removed my cuffs and closed the door before he said anything else. 'You look thin, are they feeding you well enough?'

I huffed a laugh. 'I'm eating everything they give me.'

'State-approved sandwich and an apple?' he joked along, quietly reminding me of how many versions of my prisoner persona he must have worked with during his years. 'I've been going through statements, met with a couple of people who know you personally, that sort of thing. It's slow work, but it's all coming together.'

'Who did you speak to?'

He flicked over three pages in the stack that was lying next to him. 'Truman?'

'Christ,' I said under my breath.

'And Karl? He seems like a c–'

'Cunt.'

Lucas' head snapped up and to my relief, he laughed. 'I was going to say character.'

'That too,' I agreed. 'I wouldn't ever write him though.'

'Your agent, I also spoke to him.' He folded his arms on the table in front of him then and gave me his full attention. 'He tells me that you were working on a new novel when all of this business unfolded. Is that the manuscript you asked for?' My face must have perked up. 'You want to carry on working on the book?'

'I've had a breakthrough. I'd like to be able to write.'

'I'll see what I can do, but I'm not sure where the law stands on writing and publishing from prison.'

'I'm not in prison.'

'No,' he nodded, 'no, I suppose you're not.'

A long pause stretched before I asked, 'But I will be?'

Lucas let out a curt 'Ha!' and said, 'Not if I get my way. Truman had nothing but good things to say about you, Karl less so, but as you said he seems like a... character,' he flashed me a tight smile, 'and I think that's the word we should use when we're referring to him in polite company. I've got meetings lined up with others, and I'm bringing in an associate of mine from New York to help with some of the legwork involved,' he was flicking through sheets of paper again by then, 'but until then, I want to snowball some ideas with you. So, I've got a list of possibilities here that I want to run through real fast. Consider this a... you know that game you play, to help you decide something, and you have to choose between two things as fast as you can to help you work out which ones you really want?'

I narrowed my eyes. 'Yes.'

'We're going to do that,' he said as he lifted a sheet of paper boasting a list to the top of his pile. 'Ready?'

He waited for a nod before he started.

'Noah Prescott,' he started and I felt my stomach clench, 'was he your boyfriend?'

'No.'

'Casual lover?'

'Yes.'

'Good man?'

'Good enough.'

Lucas smiled. 'Try to stick to yes or no.'

'Yes.'

'Was he a father?'

I hesitated. 'No.'

'Unfaithful to you?'

'No.'

'Jealous man?'

'No.'

'Possessive.'

'No.'

'Abusive?'

'No.'

'Never physically threatened you?'

'No.'

'Then why did you kill him?'

A hideous and uncomfortable pause elbowed its way into the room then. It was rich in damp and mildew, groaning as it moved, eventually settling on the table space between us. I leaned back in my seat to make room for it.

Lucas only smiled. 'You can't blame a guy for trying.' He screwed the sheet of paper into a tight ball and set it down on the corner to his right. 'Well, we won't be needing any of that, by the looks of things.'

I realised then that in the days when we hadn't seen each other, Lucas had been overturning rocks, peering beneath them to look for a reason or a way. I'd just scuppered his list of motives.

'Why did you ask whether Noah was a father?'

'Because it turns out he was,' he looked up and caught my

reaction, 'which was something I didn't find out until I read the police write-up about him, and given that so few people had mentioned it, news outlets included, I wondered how public that knowledge was.'

'He...' The sentence died in my mouth. My tongue felt too big, sandpaper rough and swelling still. 'May I?' I nodded towards a bottle of water that was on the table.

'Of course, of course, it's actually for you.' Lucas cracked the seal and held the opened bottle out to me. 'You can't worry about the fatherhood thing, Caroline. If you didn't know then you didn't know, and at least it wasn't any kind of a factor in your decision-making, so that's something.'

I took so many thirsty mouthfuls that my stomach hurt. When I felt the splash of fresh water against the waves in my belly I stopped drinking and set the bottle back down. I wiped my mouth clean on my wrist and answered then. 'You thought I might have killed him because he was a father?'

Lucas shrugged. 'I like to cover all of my bases.'

I lingered for a long time over whether to ask the next question or not. But some sordid part of me, hellbent on making matters worse for myself, needed to know. 'How old is his...'

'Daughter?' Lucas completed the sentence and I slow-blinked in answer. I almost didn't want to open my eyes again. 'She's three, and by all accounts he hasn't had much involvement with her. My understanding of the situation, and this is just from asking around, keep in mind – I'm yet to actually speak to the kid's mother – but my understanding is that it was a clumsy fumble some years ago that led to a very accidental pregnancy. Although how that even happens in this day and age...' Lucas trailed off and I thought I saw a soft shudder move over his shoulders. *No children waiting for you at home then.* 'Noah didn't want the kid, the mother did want the kid. It's a story as old as time. We live in the land of the free, though, so she had the baby and he stuck his head in every now and then to ease his conscience. He was paying child support, so that's a tick in his favour. I'm not sure he's necessarily the good guy in the story as a whole though, so there's that, too.'

I huffed. 'You make it sound like a good thing that he was a negligent father.'

'He was *secretive* about being a negligent father. I heard on the grapevine that he proposed to you as well, more than once?' Lucas was poised to take down any snippet of information that I might share, but I only nodded. 'It says a lot about a man, doesn't it, to propose marriage to a woman when he hasn't even told her that he's got a child waiting in the wings? Did you want children, Caroline, did you ever express that to him as something you wanted in your future?'

'No,' I stared at the table as I answered, 'it was one of the reasons my first marriage broke down. Peter, he wanted children and I... I didn't think I'd make a very good mother.'

'Did Noah know that contributed to the marriage breaking down?'

'Yes, yes, I think I told him about that.'

'And yet he was still proposing,' he repeated, more to himself than to me, as he wrote something down, 'that's interesting.' Lucas finished writing and then looked hard at me again. 'Why do you think you wouldn't make a good mother?'

I shrugged. 'I'm not a very caring person. Maternally speaking.'

Lucas bobbed his head – it was too enthusiastic to be called a nod – and he made a mm'ing noise, as though tasting something good for the first time. 'Or, you wanted to focus on your career and you were undecided about children.' He smoothed down his tie. 'The truth is malleable, Caroline. Everything is in the detailing, the phrasing. People can tolerate a career woman easier than they can tolerate a woman who isn't maternal.'

I could feel outrage simmering; something angry boiling up from my core. 'I just shot a man, Lucas,' I spat out.

'Mhmm,' he wrote something else down then, 'and I'm the man who's trying to help you get away with it...'

CHAPTER THIRTEEN

The garden at the police station was a sealed space that contained such an explosion of colour, I couldn't help but wonder which of the officers had green fingers. It must have been one of them, because a garden like that would need regular maintenance. Still, I couldn't imagine which of them cared enough for that level of commitment to a green space that I thought they must only ordinarily use for their cigarette and coffee breaks. It had been easy enough to spot that they were all smokers, bar Clarence, who had already told me explicitly that she didn't smoke because she enjoyed running too much. I remember thinking, funny, that's the same reason I never took up running – though of course, I didn't say this to her.

I've never been especially good with gardening or flowers. Peter and Joel had dealt with those areas of our marital homes. Whenever I'd lived alone, I took a great measure of pride in patio spaces and concrete slabs, which wasn't something I would ever admit to now, for fear that someone might rip them up in search of bodies.

When I was a girl, my grandmother had grown prize-winning roses, which struck me as a strange thing at the time.

Into adulthood, I came to understand that anything can be prize-winning if enough people care for it. Prior to that understanding, I would so often roll my eyes and tilt my head and trudge around the garden two steps behind my paternal grandmother, while she nipped and tucked and cut, and I collected the trimmings in a wicker basket that she'd made herself during one of her – wait for it – basket-weaving classes. Everything about it had been so painfully British.

Clarence didn't expect me to hold a basket for her. Though there were roses in this garden, that much I managed to identify. There were also bursts of turquoise and sunshine yellow and deep, deep greens, and a lush grass that looked so cushioned I often wanted to lie down on it and spot shapes in the clouds. Even on the days when the weather was appalling, and we were both wearing hideously unfashionable clear raincoats to shield ourselves, the outside space was a quiet joy where everything felt remarkably normal for thirty minutes or so – during which time we managed three laps of the square that formed the garden area. If it weren't for the handcuffs, it would have felt terribly Victorian to be taking a turn around the grounds at the start of every day.

But the walks around the garden had helped me to appreciate something else, too: Officer Clarence was quite the talker. I don't know whether it really had been that long since she'd had female company in the workplace that my presence blurred the lines of what she should and shouldn't say, but if nothing else she was a source of much needed entertainment on the days when Lucas wasn't there. She had told me she was a runner, of course; she had also mentioned that she was single, which I'd guessed, and a mother, which I'd also guessed, given that she seemed to be the only guard who gave a shit about my wellbeing – hence, the walks. And on the fifteenth walk around the gardens – there having been no walk at all the day before, on her day off – she also revealed that she's quite a reader.

'I remember my mother giving me Nancy Drew books as a child. Did you ever read Nancy Drew?' She turned to catch my reaction and I smiled, nodded. This was how she and I had come to communicate. I still wasn't ready to talk to anyone but Lucas; I'd even turned down two phone calls from Mum, though that was mostly because I couldn't stand the shame and judgement that I knew would come through the speaker. 'She gave me this battered old copy of one, *The Clue in the Crumbling Wall*, it was, and after that I was hooked. Every birthday, every Christmas, I'd always get at least one detective novel. I remember telling her that I wanted to go into police work and she laughed and said, "Of course you do."' There was a warmness to her voice as she relayed the memories, but something else around the fringes. 'I really miss her,' she added then, and I added "deceased mother" to the list of things I now knew about Officer Clarence. 'Anyway, my real reason for mentioning this is because, now this is super weird and I'm sure the fellas would *roast* me for it if they knew I was doing this, but on my day off yesterday I absolutely blitzed through *'Til Death.*'

My head snapped up. *My book?*

'I know, I know, it's weird!' She held her hands up in defence. 'But I couldn't help myself. I heard on the grapevine that you're a writer, like an *actual* writer, not the types of writers you get at Jerry's reading circle, and I thought, I'll be damned, I can't not.'

The double negative got stuck in my teeth. And I had questions about Jerry and his reading circle. Were they looking for guest authors? Could I get a day release for that sort of thing? I huffed a laugh at the thought and carried on walking in time with her. *'Til Death* was my debut, and it wasn't my finest work, but I was keen to hear her thoughts all the same. The plot revolved around a man who had been diagnosed with cancer two years before the story begins. After a long-standing battle against illness and treatment alike, he finally admits defeat, refuses treatment, and prepares himself for the inevitable. His poor wife is taken along on this journey with him, and it's when he's "preparing for the inevitable" that she becomes a key player in the narrative rather than a side character. I wondered what a sentimental police officer would have to say about a woman who helped her husband die.

'The writing is *beautiful*, Caroline, it really is; you have such a way with words.'

Normally I would have thanked her for the compliment. That's what we writers do, when someone parts our arse cheeks and blows smoke up into us. We thank them and, if we try *really* hard, we sometimes even manage to blush, and we definitely try to bat the compliment away, too, with comments like, 'You're too kind!' and 'Really, the book tells itself!'. This way, though, I could just enjoy the rain shower of pleasantries – which, to no surprise, I much preferred. She waxed lyrical about the book for a full ten minutes, a whole turn around the garden, telling me how gruelling the treatment process is in my descriptions, how tired the male character sounds, how strong his relationship is with his wife, and I nodded along with each point. Then, we arrived at the unavoidable.

'Though of course, I'm not sure I could have killed him myself.'

Ah, the moral high ground.

There was a long pause after she said this, and I couldn't decide whether she was re-thinking the sentiment, or whether it had just hit her square in the face that she'd told a murderer she wasn't sure whether she could kill a man. I bit back on a laugh, tucking my lips into my mouth to hide the signs of it. I kept my head bowed and my arms loose in front of me while she thought about her comment.

'Actually, Christ, I don't know. If it was someone I loved, is it *worse* to watch them suffer all that time? I really don't... I dunno whether I have *that* in me, either. It's such an ugly balance of... crap, and now I've said it, I don't know. I could fall either way, maybe, depending on how bad or for how long they'd... well, suffered. And it's hard to see another human being suffering and elect *not* to do anything about it, right? I think I became a cop exactly so that *didn't* happen.' She was having a conversation with herself by this point and I could only let her roll with it, all the while a snaking sense of satisfaction coiled loosely in my belly that it was my work causing this ethical eruption. And then, I did allow myself to smile. 'You probably think I'm ridiculous, dancing around a minefield of decisions that I don't actually have to make,' she paused to laugh, though it was a self-conscious sound, 'but good writing makes you think, doesn't it? And I guess what I'm saying is your book made me think, do I have it in me to kill someone? If it helps them?' She hurried to add this last part, as though realising her potential blunder. 'It's a hard question for anyone to ask themselves, isn't it?' She turned to face me then, as we came to a stop at the entryway to the police building.

It looked as though she was waiting for an actual answer, having forgotten the vow of silence somewhere during her review of my work. But I only shrugged and turned to face the door, as though signalling the end of our discussion, and she said, 'Of course, of course,' before hurrying to open up the back entrance. She was right, obviously, it was a hard question to answer – and the book was designed to at the very least make people wonder. But I was long past the point in my life where I felt entitled to wonder whether I might one day kill a man – whether it was mercy or murder hardly mattered now.

TALK TRUE CRIME TO ME
EPISODE 381

Release date: July 2015

Darla: Hello and welcome to another episode of *Talk True Crime To Me,* the podcast dedicated to true crime literature in its many forms. I'm Darla and I'm here with my co-host Eddie. Eddie, go ahead and say hello to everyone.

Eddie: Hello.

Darla: [Laughter] Eddie is in a grump with me this week because I've made him read something that isn't true crime, but it *is* something written by a true criminal.

Eddie: Is she still getting paid royalties? That's what I wanna know.

Darla: I mean, I guess? The books aren't about the crime she's *just* committed, so why shouldn't she be getting paid for her hard work?

Eddie: [Pause] I can't believe you're even fucking asking me that.

Darla: [Laughter] The first fuck of the show!

Eddie: Come on! This woman shoots a man in cold blood and you go ahead and make me *buy* one of her novels.

Darla: But was it, or was it not, a good fucking novel?

Eddie: [Pause] Fine, whatever, it was a good fucking novel, but I still have torn up feelings about this whole thing, Darla. Listeners, in case you didn't guess it already, Darla's book choice for this episode was *Road Rage* by Caroline Geel and it's a book about a woman who kills someone.

Darla: That is such an understatement and you are such a whiner. Okay, *Road Rage* is a book about a woman in England who has this whopper of a blowout bust-up with her husband, and she goes for a drive to cool off. But while she's driving down this super windy country road with her foot on the gas, she smashes into someone who's walking at night which, red flag, that person might have been a serial killer anyway–

Eddie: Only, they weren't. They were a totally innocent bystander, they got crushed by a car, and then the woman spends the rest of the novel covering up her crime by committing *more* crimes, and then framing her husband for the hit and run.

Darla: And listeners, let me tell you, this is some tense shit from page one. Even the relationship between husband and wife is fishy here, right, because–

Eddie: Because the book was written by a murderer, is that why it's fishy, Darla?

CHAPTER FOURTEEN

The inevitable had happened: they had moved me to a jail, and I did not care for it. I was sharing a cell with a beautiful black woman who I guessed was twenty years my senior, if not more. She was blissfully silent and known to everyone, it seemed, as Ma – not that I needed to know her name, on account of not swapping a word with her. She wasn't the problem. Ma only said morning to me at the start of every day and goodnight at the end. Meanwhile, the rest of the women did not stop fucking talking – no matter the time of day. The entire place was a constant rumble of chatter, accusations and threats. And no matter the lengths I went to, to keep my head down, there would be a time in every single given day when one woman would recognise me – as though having only just realised I was there – as the white Brit who'd offed a man right in front of a room full of people.

'You must have balls the size of footballs to do that.'

'You must be dumb as fuck to do that.'

'You musta been asking for trouble to do it that way.'

Balls the size of footballs, dumb as fuck and asking for trouble, that's me.

Jail, allegedly, wasn't built for people who had committed serious crimes. That was what prisons were for. Yet, I was far from being the only murderer stashed inside these walls. I wondered whether they slipped us all in during the dead of night, hoping no one would realise that a family of women all capable of killing someone had been given free rein to scheme and share notes. But of course, like a true family, what we actually did was avoid talking to each other at all costs, with every faction of the jail having *their* murderer, or murderers in some cases, who they pledged allegiance to, without showing much interest in another group's killer. I was the white women's murderer – but the other white women, there for petty theft, carjacking and minor offences relating to the drug trade, technically hadn't adopted me yet. I was a lone predator still, and that was fine.

The guards there were different, too. To start with, at least two of them were definitely having "inappropriate relations" with a number of prisoners. I hadn't seen anything with my own eyes, but I'd heard women comparing notes – because it seemed even in jail there were still women who were desperate to talk about their sex lives. I'd settled for masturbating once to the dulcet tones of Ma snoring beneath me, and even then it had been as a sleeping aid. There were also the guards who were definitely bringing drugs into the place – the greatest prison cliché – and there was one, and only one, who seemed to actually want to befriend us all. I avoided that man at all costs. Frankly, Officer Clarence at the local station had been friendly contact enough and I felt as though I'd hit my quota of prison officials who were trying to make my life easier. Granted, I didn't want them to make my life any harder, either. But if I were given an option as to which type of guard I wanted to spend time with, then I had to admit it was probably time to try hard drugs.

Another observation I'd made about jail was that time seemed to move in an entirely different way. We were kicked out of our bunks early to breakfast, early to lunch, early to dinner and then inevitably locked in again. I was lying on my top bunk thinking of Noah, enjoying the loudness that filtered in through the open door, when Ma walked in one day and announced that she couldn't believe it was only eleven in the morning still. I was stunned on two levels. First, I was sure we'd already had lunch – but was that the day before? Second, I was sure it was the longest sentence I'd heard her string together. She landed heavily on the mattress beneath my elevated one and the metal of the frame creaked under her weight.

'It's been a week now,' she announced, and my eyes widened when I realised of course, she must be talking to me. 'How you holding up?

I heard the bed shift again and I imagined her lifting her legs, settling in.

I went back and forth on whether to answer. The thought of speaking was easier now, less uncomfortable. And while I wasn't exactly in the market for a friend, I reasoned in those seconds of dead air that if I were going to open up to anyone, it should probably be someone who at least seemed to have prison clout. 'I'm getting by,' I said, then, 'I'm just trying to keep my head down.'

She laughed. 'Easier said than done in this place.'

I wasn't sure whether that marked the end of the conversation or not. But given that Ma had been kind enough to make the offer of talking, I felt compelled to keep things afloat further. Americans didn't seem to have that same level of social courtesy that I had since come to understand as being another quintessentially British thing, but still, even under the circumstances, I couldn't resist the pull of it.

'What are you in for?' I asked then, because I'd heard it said, read it written, in so many fictionalised accounts of prisons before. It was, I assumed, a natural thing to ask of someone. Though it felt a little like asking someone's age, or their weight.

'Assault.'

I took note of the fact that she hadn't asked me in return why I was there.

'My daughter stole some money from me so I slapped her around a little.'

'How much did she steal?'

'$248.'

It seemed an oddly specific amount. But arguably worth slapping someone around for.

'For drugs, too,' she added, which I thought gave Ma even greater justification. 'No sense in asking what you're in for, is there, Princess Di?'

Princess Diana and I had nothing in common apart from misguided decision-making when it came to husbands. She and I certainly didn't look alike: her with her iconic blonde short style; me with my reckless red waves that I was just about managing to squeeze into a hairband these days, such was their wildness without access to the right hair products. Points of difference aside, though, Di and I did have another common thread to our bows: we were both British. That was enough to equate sameness, I guessed.

'I think everyone in here knows why I'm here, yes,' I answered.

There was a long pause then, when again I thought the conversation might have ended without me quite realising it. But then Ma added, 'Think that's the reason people are giving you your space, girlie.'

'Because I killed a man?'

'No, because no one knows *why* you killed a man.' Another pause elbowed between us after that: one, two, three, I counted the seconds in time with my breathing. 'Girls in here killed a man but at least they had their reasons, and Lord, if they won't sit and tell you about them to no end as though they're auditioning for the cast of *Chicago*.' I stifled a laugh, both at the reference and at the fact that in my mind Ma was an entirely unlikely audience for the show. 'But there's something to be said for a woman who kills a man without reason.'

'I had my reasons,' I lied.

'You just don't feel like telling anybody?'

'I guess not.'

'Your lawyer know?'

'Nope.'

'Shit.' She made a noise then, a kissing sound. 'How's he defending you?'

'Beats me.'

A harsh 'Ha!' drifted up from her. 'Well we got that in common, girlie. Bad, bad men defending bad, bad women, hm.'

'He isn't a bad lawyer. I just... I just don't know how he'll defend me,' I admitted.

'See, mine is just bad. Public, though. ' She made the same kissing sound again. 'I guess yours isn't?'

Lucas was far from what I imagined the State would have provided me with when it came to legal representation. I was seeing him more regularly than any public defender would have managed either, I guessed. He hadn't visited me since I'd been in jail, but I thought that was less about the change in location and more about the time-consuming endeavour of looking at my case from every awkward angle in the hope of finding something he might defend until the end of a day in court. In a strange way, I was missing him – or perhaps, missing the company of someone who didn't have a legal record.

'No, he's not public.'

'Expensive?'

'You bet,' I lied again, albeit by a technicality. Lucas *was* expensive, Ma was right. But Lucas was also working my case pro bono now. He'd told me that two visits ago and when I asked why, he'd only laughed and shaken his head, as though he couldn't quite believe the question. I'd ruminated on that a lot since. Was it publicity? Was he really *that* fond of me? It seemed more likely to be the former. I didn't know how much airtime the case was getting exactly, but I would have bet Lucas' retainer again that he was getting enough time in front of a microphone and a set of cameras to make working with me worth it.

'It'll be worth it though, assuming I make it out of here.'

'Oh, girlie, you'll make it outta here, just a case of where you go.'

'Isn't that life all over?'

'Hm,' she dragged the noise out, 's'pose.'

'How long have you been in jail, Ma?'

'This time?'

I had to swallow another laugh before it erupted. 'Yes.'

'Twenty months.'

'Twenty months awaiting trial?' I couldn't keep the shock out of my voice. Lucas had warned me that things moved slowly. Were trial dates scheduled according to the severity of a crime? I wondered. It seemed like something I should have researched myself before all this started. Did murder mean you could queue jump the judicial system – or did it mean everything took that bit longer still, because you were probably here for life anyway? I felt each word in every wonder like a small, sharp needle slipping into my chest, and I realised then that my breathing had accelerated, too. I closed my eyes and rested my hands on my stomach and concentrated hard on not making myself a weak animal in an enclosure full of wild ones. And in doing so, I missed Ma's answer, even though somewhere in the well of me, I thought I likely knew what it was. 'Sorry,' I said, making a conscious effort to keep a tremor from my voice, 'I missed that.'

'I only said yeah.'

Twenty months awaiting trial. I swallowed each word and felt them drop, a pellet at a time, into my stomach, and I felt the ripples move out and through me. Then I thought of the manuscript in the safe at home, the one that Lucas still hadn't brought me. I thought of the legal pads I'd requested three, maybe four times now, that still hadn't materialised. And in the background, like an advertising jingle playing in sinister tones, I thought of the unbearable possibility that I might have to wait that long and longer to tell my story.

CHAPTER FIFTEEN

Somehow, I arrived at the interview room before Lucas did. I'd been sitting there tapping my handcuffs against the metal table for nearly five minutes – I had nothing to do nowadays but count time – when he walked in, huffing and cursing underneath his breath. He threw a chocolate bar on the tabletop and turned to the guard who was still lingering at the door – 'I want these cuffs off my client before you leave.' Then he took his seat opposite me. When we were alone, he ferreted around inside his briefcase until there was a fresh pad and what looked like a new pen – I'd noticed that Lucas was a lid-chewer, but this one looked unbitten still – sitting between us. He nudged the chocolate bar towards me.

'Honestly, the lengths a man has to go to these days to smuggle chocolate into a jail, and yet somehow they've just had an inmate taken to the county hospital for a drug overdose. Jesus.' He ran a hand through his hair, pushing the mop of brown away from his face, and as though noticing it for the first time I saw then how clean his jawline was, how neat. 'I'm convinced you're not eating properly while you're in here. You aren't on a hunger strike?' he asked with the same narrow-eyed expression my mother gave me when she thought I was developing an eating disorder at thirteen. I shook my head and frowned. 'Will you eat the chocolate bar anyway, for me?' His tone was pleading, as though he truly thought I might resist the offer. But of course I wouldn't. My metabolism had evolved into something untameable since that afternoon at the hotel and I would have happily sucked Lucas's fingers clean of Cheetos stains if it meant an extra taste of something. Though I tried not to linger on that thought for too long as I tore into the chocolate and took the first bite.

'Happy?'

'Incredibly.' Lucas folded his arms and rested them on the table. 'How are you?'

'I share a cell with a lady called Ma, who's in here for slapping her daughter around.'

Lucas squinted, nodded. 'Did the daughter deserve it?'

I took a second bite and shrugged. 'Some would argue yes.'

'Well, Ma clearly thought so.' He leaned in further, closing some of the distance between us. He looked to be relaxing into the meeting a little easier now the great chocolate heist had passed. 'But how *are* you? Seriously, are they treating you okay?'

'Generally, I'd say so,' I shrugged again, 'it's jail, isn't it? They're not here to be friends with me, they're here to make sure I don't make it back into the general population. And the women are fine. I'm keeping my head down; they're mostly leaving me alone. I suspect that Ma has something to do with it.'

'Well,' he started to move papers around, 'as long as you aren't her bitch.'

The comment caught me so off-guard that a howl of laughter erupted out of me, and Lucas seemed genuinely delighted by my reaction.

'Now we've got the pleasantries out of the way. Can we...' He held up a sheet that was adorned with notes and scribbles by way of finishing the sentence and I nodded. 'I've had a chat with Joel recently. He's a decent enough guy, right?' He looked up to catch my answer.

'Sure, I guess.'

'He gave you the gun, didn't he?'

I narrowed my eyes. 'It was a Welcome to the States present.'

'And he took you to the shooting range?'

'Yes.'

'Made sure you knew what you were doing when it came to firing, reloading, the lot?'

I nodded, slowly. 'Yes.'

'Why was that, do you think?'

'He told me he wanted me to feel safe. I asked why I wouldn't feel safe and he shrugged,' I paused to dredge up the right details of the memory, 'he shrugged and said sometimes women don't feel safe, and everyone has a gun here anyway.'

'Different culture to back home?'

'Handguns aren't exactly readily available in the UK.'

'And what was it like, carrying a gun around with you?'

'I didn't carry a gun around with me.' He frowned, and his lips puckered, and I realised my error. 'Before that day, I didn't carry a gun around with me.'

'I think you did.'

And he sounded so certain it crossed my mind that maybe he knew something I didn't.

'I think you were in a new country, on your own, maybe not to begin with because you had Joel, but after a time, you were on your own. You're a vulnerable woman, and Maine has nothing in place to say you can't carry a concealed weapon, nothing to say that what you did was wrong, in taking that weapon out with you. So I think you took it that day, and you took it every now and then before that day, too. Not to work, not to school.

But when you were walking alone, socially, I think you carried a gun.'

'Lucas, I don't think I understand what–'

'I don't think you planned to take a gun out with you that afternoon.'

It was a crash of pennies then; one after the other tumbling off the edge of a slider.

'I don't think,' Lucas started again, 'that it was premeditated.'

'I understand.'

'I don't think it was unusual for you to carry a gun with you.'

'It wasn't,' I agreed, 'because I'm a vulnerable woman in a country I don't know well, and I wanted to feel protected sometimes.'

Lucas smiled. 'I suspected as much.' He drew what looked like a big tick alongside a cluster of bullet points and I wondered whether we'd just built the first wall of my defence. 'The other good news here is that Joel is willing to testify to having gifted you the gun, helped train you up in using it, but he's also happy to be a character witness. Nothing but good things to say about you, it seems, and that never hurts in a trial like this. Do you...' he paused to glance over the sheet, 'no, nothing else there.' He looked at me then and smiled. 'Do you have any questions or reservations about what we've covered there?'

'None at all.'

'Glad to hear it.' Lucas turned the sheet over to reveal another well-scribbled one. 'Next on the agenda. Peter.'

'What *about* Peter?'

'When did you last speak?'

I tried hard to think of the last conversation, but the brain is adept at blocking out trauma. 'I honestly don't know. I think... I think at some point after the divorce I made a drunken phone call, to tell him I missed him.' Have we spoken since then, though? 'I can't recall what his reaction was.'

Lucas waved the comment away. 'Happens to the best of us. But I take it you aren't on good terms?' I felt something pull in my face and he noticed it, too. 'He isn't exactly shying away from the odd interview here and there, and we need to do some damage control against that.' His pen hovered over the page that was already full of scribblings; I wondered how there could possibly be room for more. 'What was your marriage like?'

'In the beginning, ideal.'

'In the middle?'

'Uncomfortable.'

'At the end?'

'Horrific.'

'Okay, give me specifics. Any abuse?'

There was a stand-out argument towards the end of the marriage. Peter and I had been at a local schools event. It was meant to be networking-meets-socialising, but as soon as the sun dipped the teachers in the room turned into drunken animals – such is our way. Peter and I had both had too much to drink, and that's when he overheard me telling a mutual friend that we were having some problems, as a couple. He'd yanked me away from the woman in question and pulled me into a dark corner like a parent ready to reprimand a teenager who they'd caught smoking for the first time. It wasn't anyone else's business what was happening between us, he'd told me. Though of course, his drunken whisper hadn't been as quiet as he'd originally thought. There was a cluster of onlookers who not only looked shocked by Peter's tone, but also by the tightening grip he'd held around my upper arm; a vice tethering me to him, stopping me from drifting away and opening my mouth to others. We'd gone home shortly after that and the argument had continued. Like all drunken arguments, it escalated past the point that had started it, and before we knew it we weren't only arguing about the party but about the writing and the lack of children and the financial problems and then–

'He hit me, once.'

–I'd hit him.

'Context?'

'We were drunk and arguing; it was nothing.'

'It was something,' Lucas answered, with the stern set expression of a man who obviously couldn't stand the thought of someone hitting a woman. His face alone was almost enough to make me feel guilty for the lie – almost. Not guilty enough to retract the remark, though. 'Did you ever tell anyone?'

I shook my head. 'It never seemed worth mentioning.'

'Well,' he wrote something down, 'now it's an ace in our pocket.'

Lucas and I went back and forth for nearly an hour after that. We discussed Peter more, then my mother, then my father – and his suicide, as though the two things were an inextricable pairing. And then before I knew it he was packing his things back into his briefcase. I was desperate for a normal interaction with him then. I wanted to ask what his plans were for the rest of the day, or whether he knew what he was going to have for dinner that evening. I wasn't sure whether it was a kind of transference that was happening, or whether I would have been desperate for this contact with anyone besides Ma.

'Before I go,' he was smoothing the lapels on his jacket, readying himself for any cameras that might be outside, I thought, 'you'll be getting another visitor tomorrow. Her name is Melinda Ronan; she's a psychiatrist.'

I nodded. I knew this was coming. 'What do you want me to tell her?'

Lucas's brow pulled together in what looked like genuine confusion. 'Be honest.'

Easier said than done.

CHAPTER SIXTEEN

There were no two ways of saying it: Melinda Ronan was an offensively attractive woman. If someone were drafting a screenplay of this debacle, she was exactly the sort of woman who would have been cast in the role of the psychiatrist. She had thick blonde hair that was pulled back into a complicated bun, giving space to her perfectly smooth and made-up face. Her blending was commendable, with not a foundation line in sight, and she'd paired that with a nude lipstick and a slim lick of mascara that gave her a wide-eyed expression, magnified by the simple black bottle-top glasses. She was wearing a skirt suit in black, tailored to fit and definitely not store bought, and beneath that was a loose-fitting pale pink blouse. Melinda was the type of thin that meant it didn't matter how baggy her clothes might be, you could still tell there was a petite woman underneath them. I'd noticed when she stood to shake my hand, and then slipped her jacket off her shoulders and onto the back of the chair before sitting down again. We were in a different interview room to the one that Lucas and I had shared, but it was still as State-approved; still within earshot of the howling beasts I spent my days with now. I couldn't help but wonder how out of place Melinda must have felt. Will you dry clean that suit when you leave here? Go home and immediately shower us all off? I could have been wrong, of course, and perhaps she did this sort of thing all the time, but something about her awkwardly perching on the edge of her chair made me doubt it. Melinda had a leatherbound notebook on the table in front of her, a pen, and two bottles of water.

'For you,' she said, pushing one of them slightly closer to me.

'Thank you.'

'It can be thirsty work, all the talking.' She smiled, shuffled in her seat, and picked up her pen. 'I think Mr Williams will have already told you a little about me, but just in case, I'm Dr Ronan,' she fumbled, 'though you already know that from the handshake. You're welcome to call me Melinda. In fact, I think I'd prefer it. Do you mind me calling you Caroline?' I shook my head: no. 'Okay, Caroline, all I want to do today is have a talk with you. We'll have a talk, you'll answer some questions, and there may be a second part to this further down the line, if that's okay with you as well? Then I'll prepare a report, and Mr Williams will take it from there. Does all of that sound okay?'

Am I even allowed to say no? I nodded. 'Of course.'

'So, I hear you're a writer?'

It seemed an odd place to start, but I leaned in. 'I was, before this.'

Melinda smiled. 'You still are. Did you always want to be a writer?'

'Apart from five minutes during my teenage years when I wanted to be a surgeon.'

'What made you think otherwise?'

'I'm terrible at science.' I smiled. 'And I hate blood.'

'Still, being a writer must take a lot of work, right? I definitely couldn't write how you write. It's fiction, isn't it?'

I narrowed my eyes. 'Mostly. I've written a few essays along the way.'

'And what's your fiction about?'

I hesitated. 'Crimes, of a sort.'

'Not quite conventional crime then?'

'Not quite shooting a man in the chest in a room full of people.'

Melinda made an awkward noise. 'You don't waste time.'

'It's the journalist in me, always getting to the heart of a story.'

'Do you want to talk about Noah?'

I didn't know whether it was a trick question. Yes, and I might seem too keen. No, and I might seem like I was avoiding something. 'I don't know, if I'm honest. I feel...' I let the sentence die while I tried to work out an authentic end for it. 'I feel like I'm being tested here.'

'Here, in this room?' I dipped my head in answer. 'Caroline, to be clear, I'm not trying to trip you up. I don't work for the court. I only work for Mr Williams insofar as he's the one who'll cash my invoice,' she half-laughed, 'but I am solely here for you, just to talk. There aren't right or wrong answers to anything we're going to discuss today. Okay?'

'Okay,' I agreed, even though I thought it was all bullshit.

'Take me all the way back, to the young girl who wanted to be a writer.' She smiled and the expression seemed authentic on her, as though she actually thought this might be safe ground. 'What was that girl like?'

Melinda made notes throughout, even though it didn't feel like I'd told her anything that was particularly noteworthy. It took me twenty minutes to tell her I'd had a relatively happy childhood, despite my father's regular stints with depression that resulted in his suicide. When I said that part, she looked as though I'd slapped her.

'He killed himself?'

I nodded.

'That can't have been easy for you.' She seemed genuinely interested. 'What was life like after that, can you remember?'

In truth, there wasn't much I could remember. For a long time it felt as though I had shifted from taking care of Dad – who wouldn't even shower himself by the end – to taking care of Mum, who seemed sincerely stunned that her husband, the man who had battled depression for his entire adult life, had finally thrown in the towel. I was less surprised than she was, I'd always thought, but then maybe I'd been close enough to see it coming.

'Life just carried on,' I shrugged. 'It does when someone dies, doesn't it?'

Melinda seemed to spend a long time writing after that and I wondered whether I'd said something, or said too much even, but it was too late to draw it all back in now. I could only hold my breath, and my tongue, while I waited for the next question.

'Have you ever suffered from depression?'

I hesitated. 'Hasn't everyone at some point?'

'Do you believe that?'

'I think I do, yeah. But there are different types of depression, aren't there? There's the depression where you go through a blue period and come out the other side. And then,' I lingered over how to explain the unexplainable, 'and then there's the depression where you live in a colour chart, made up singularly of the colour blue, in differing shades and hues. Dad was the latter of the two, obviously.'

'But you're the former?'

I nodded. 'I like to think so.'

'Have you ever experienced any other mental health difficulties?'

'No.'

'That's a very firm answer,' she observed with a smile again.

I didn't know what to say to that. I didn't believe that I'd suffered any mental health difficulties. But I was also acutely aware, still, of a conversation Peter and I had had once where he'd gently laid a hand on my forearm, looked at me with doe eyes, and softly said, 'I honestly think there's something wrong with you, Caroline.' The comment came after Dad had died, maybe a year after, and it was accompanied by a fumbling explanation wherein Peter had explained he didn't think I was grieving properly – though he also couldn't explain what grief looked like, exactly, as though trying to explain the face of someone he once knew personally, but now wouldn't recognise walking down the street. I hadn't done anything with the comment, or the conversation, only carried it in my back pocket – ready, it seemed, to overanalyse in a setting such as this.

'I just don't think there's anything wrong with me.'

Melinda drew in a deep breath and asked, 'So why did you shoot Noah?'

Despite knowing that we would have to come around to this topic, the question still caught me by surprise. My mouth bobbed open as though I had an answer at the ready, and perhaps part of my brain did, but it certainly wasn't a part of my brain that was in friendly communication with my mouth. All that I managed was hot, dead air.

'That was unfair. There was a better way to ask that,' she admitted. 'But do you think it's a normal thing, for one person to shoot another?'

'In the right circumstances.'

'And those are?'

'Self-defence, mostly.'

'Is that how you see what happened with Noah?'

'No, it wasn't self-defence. Besides, even if Noah had been being violent, he didn't have a gun. So, my having a gun wouldn't have been fair anyway.' I tried to weigh every word carefully, self-conscious in my pseudo confessions to her. I was terrified she would take something away from this that I hadn't been ready to give. 'You don't take a gun to a fist fight, do you?'

'No,' she nodded slowly, 'no, I suppose you don't. Was Noah ever violent, though?'

'No, never.' I huffed a laugh. 'I distinctly remember me stepping on a spider in my living room one evening and him being outraged, because of the sheer aggression of it.'

She wrote something down then asked, 'Do you think of yourself as aggressive?'

'Only when it comes to spiders.'

'But otherwise?'

'Otherwise, no. I saw Dad hit Mum once when I was a kid and I promised that I'd never been that person.' Apart from that one time with Peter, I taunted myself, but at least the truth of that didn't slip out. 'It was only one time with Dad, too,' I rushed to add, realising I'd left that particular memory out of the happy home portrait I'd painted already.

'Could we pause this for a second, Caroline?' She was pushing back from the table already. 'Apologies, too much water and I desperately need the bathroom.'

Paranoia kicked in and I spent five minutes after that imagining her having a hurried phone conversation with Lucas where she explained that I was certifiably crazy and he should have nothing more to do with me. Though I hadn't thought too seriously until now about what his reaction to that advice might be, if someone official were to tell him I really was undefendable: abandon all hope, ye who offer counsel.

'That's much better,' she said as she slipped back into the room, and I felt my worries ebb with her arrival. I could keep them at bay if I could only keep busy. 'I didn't realise how much time had passed though, Caroline, and I'm afraid we are going to have to spill this into more than one session, which I've cleared with Mr Williams already.' So she *had* called him while she was outside? Something clicked in the back of my brain and I felt my head twitch with it. 'But I want to swing back to something I've already asked, because I don't know that I handled it all that well the first time. If you'll indulge me?'

'Okay,' I answered, sounding every bit as sullen as I felt.

'Why do you think you did it? Why do you think you shot Noah?'

I noticed the difference in her phrasing now, to when she asked before. There was something more careful about it, so I tried to match the care with my answer. I tipped my head back to stare hard at the ceiling for a second, and avoid the hot glare of Melinda, who I imagined was already drafting her research paper about all of this.

'I wanted to know what it was like to shoot a man.'

I glanced at her then, in time to see her head bob and her eyes narrow. 'Why?'

'Haven't you ever wanted to know?'

And the way she paused made me wonder whether she was really considering it.

CHAPTER SEVENTEEN

Jail quickly taught me that desperate times often lead to desperate measures. *My* desperate measure was Officer Friendly. Having written him off as someone who was only terrible at being a stern prison guard, there were many occasions when I was in the same open space as him without even registering his existence. But then, there were exceptions to that, too. It was during one of these exceptions that I was watching him talk to another inmate – tall, blonde and exhausted, I had no idea who she was or why she was there – and I saw her laugh, touch his arm, as though flirting in the wild, and then drop her hand nearby to where his own was, resting by his side. That's when I saw it: the gold foil of a chocolate bar passing from his hand to hers. He was smuggling loot into the jail, I realised then, and in synchronicity with that, I realised how useful having a friend like him might be.

Lucas still hadn't given me access to the manuscript that was locked in my safe at home. Though now I was here, under my own lock and key, I didn't know how much access he would even be able to provide. It was a heft of paper that he was unlikely to smuggle in and I was even less likely to be able to hide. A legal pad though, I could hide... a legal pad or two, I could sleep on. And I was willing to bet that I knew enough of the story still to continue with the book from here, even without reminding myself of the previous chapters. It may have been an inane and strange thing to preoccupy myself with, given the circumstances. But time was rolling at varying speeds from day to day, hour to hour even, and my desperation was a physical weight on me by then, something tied around my neck in a firm knot, pulling me down to a seabed. Besides which, I reasoned it couldn't hurt to have a friend with benefits – benefits like a pen, or the occasional chocolate bar.

'Sir?' I caught his attention one afternoon.

Officer Friendly – Officer Clifton according to his name badge, which I was for the first time close enough to see – must have been a similar age to me. There was a speckled grey patterning appearing throughout his dark brown, nearly black hair, and there were freckles across his nose that I hadn't noticed before either. He smiled with teeth that suggested he was perhaps paid better than I would have guessed prison guards were – either that, or he had a side hustle beyond the walls and barbed wire. His full cheeks puckered around his mouth into something that looked like dimples, though they weren't quite right, and I tried not to let the creasing distract me as I worked to pull my own face into a matching greeting: wide smile, doe eyes.

'How can I help you, inmate?'

'Caroline, please,' I answered, my voice low to shut out any listeners-in. I'd heard him call some of the other women by their first names, so I knew he wasn't morally opposed to it. Besides, if you couldn't be on a first-name basis with someone who you were risking your livelihood for, then what did that say? He nodded in answer to what I'd said, but I noticed the smile lessened slightly, giving way to something like confusion, or maybe even suspicion. 'Can I talk to you about... well, about some struggles I'm having?'

The smile fell to a frown of concern. 'Is someone giving you a hard time?'

'No, no, absolutely not,' I rushed an answer, 'it's just... I suppose *being* here is.'

His head bobbed and I wondered how many times he must have heard this particular sob story. 'It's a difficult adjustment period, I can imagine, and you're new here still, aren't you? It's been... what?'

I'm not even sure, I admitted to myself, though it was too sad to admit aloud. Instead, I shrugged and said, 'Only a little while.'

'Still, if you're having wellbeing problems–'

'It isn't that, even. It's just, I suppose, there are certain things that would make life a little easier around here, and I don't know how to go about getting them.' I looked up at him from under hooded eyes and I hoped the expression was a sultry one. 'I don't even mean what you probably think I mean,' I said with a light laugh sitting on the fringes of my voice: playful; innocent; absolutely not after drugs or whatever you might need to make hooch.

'Okay.' He adjusted his position, leaned back on the wall and folded both arms. 'Well, what is it you're looking for, exactly?'

I tipped my head forward and spoke softly. 'A pen.'

A curt laugh erupted out of him that caught the attention of two other women. They eyed us both for a second before going back to their conversation.

'A pen? Like, to write with?'

'I don't know whether you know, but before... all this,' I tripped up on how to phrase the before period but he didn't flicker with discomfort and that was a relief, 'before, I was a writer. I still am a writer, and I'm in the middle of a book, and I can't get to the blasted thing, and if I could only have paper, and a pen, maybe, access to the library even, I know it'd be the most helpful thing in the world.'

I'd heard the prison had a library, though not many people seemed to make use of it – not least because it was a protected area, and visiting there was a privilege I hadn't graduated to yet. But I thought that if Officer Friendly were feeling particularly generous then maybe, just *maybe*, I could sidestep Lucas altogether and work on the novel whether he liked it or not. He hadn't forbidden it, as such, but he certainly didn't seem to be encouraging it. Not that I needed encouragement by then; I'd spent so many hours staring at the writing as it laid itself bare on the wall of my cell, I had all the momentum I needed. I just didn't have the fucking paper.

Friendly stared off into the distance for a while and narrowed his eyes. I followed his glare. It was so intently fixed that I was convinced he must be looking at something a mere mortal like myself simply couldn't see. When I followed the sightline back to his expression, I saw he'd fixed me with a similar stare then.

'Can I trust you?' he asked, pointedly.

I shrugged. 'I don't see why you wouldn't be able to trust me.' I had to hope that the dead man and the gun wouldn't be brought up as part of this exchange. 'After all, how much damage can one woman possibly do in a library?' I forced a coy laugh and he smiled, which told me everything I needed to know about how well-read he wasn't.

'If I get you library access, would that...'

I wasn't sure what the end of the sentence was. *Would that mean you owe me? Would that put you in my debt?* Of everything I'd heard about Officer Friendly so far, none of it suggested he was in the business of exchanging favours. But I wouldn't have been able to blame the man if he was. He held the proverbial keys to a kingdom of sweets, hair products, and in my case, library access. And by then I was already certain that an incarcerated criminal would do nearly anything for their luxury of choice. Will I have sex with this man, if that's what it comes to? I wondered, as I watched him tilt his head to one side. Of course I will.

'Would that make your life in here a bit easier?'

My head jerked back at the question. It was more straightforward than I'd thought it would be. 'Yes, infinitely so.'

He nodded. 'Okay, well, let me see what I can do. You're a new inmate and all, so you shouldn't really... but then... Okay, sure, let me see what I can do.' He flashed me a smile that seemed to be genuine. I took a quick scan of his teeth to see if there was anything stuck between them: suspicion; malice; a willingness to double-cross me somehow. But there was only a small flourish of green – lettuce, I guessed, from whatever he'd inhaled for lunch. I thought of asking him what the chances were of him smuggling me in a vegetable that hadn't been blanched with heat, or cooked by someone who ordinarily I wouldn't even have shaken hands with, but I didn't want to push my luck.

'You have no idea what you've just done,' I answered with an equally wide smile. 'Honestly, Officer, thank you, thank you ever so much.' I backed away with my hands clasped as though in mock prayer, and then I hurried home to my cell before the good Officer Friendly could change his mind.

It took two days to grant the library access. By all accounts it wasn't easy, but as Friendly led me into the library for the first time, he informed me that the look on my face was reward enough for the effort he'd gone to. I managed not to vomit in my mouth, and only thanked him again for the work he'd put into making this happen. Then, he produced the real sweetener on

the deal. Friendly ferreted around in the pocket of his trousers –
"Something else you'll be needing," – and I felt my stomach
snatch in mild panic. Maybe there *is* a catch... But seconds later
he pulled out a pen, and flashed me another winning smile. 'I
can't let you leave here with this, obviously, because that thing
in here is basically a deadly weapon,' a nervous laugh broke
apart his sentence, 'but if you hand it in whenever you leave,
then it's yours for the taking for the time that you're in here.'

I snatched the biro. 'You're too good to me, you really are.'

A pale blush moved across his cheeks and in the harsh
lighting it was impossible not to notice. For extra impact, I gave
his forearm a soft squeeze in the same way I'd seen another
inmate do, and then I smiled again.

'Well, get writing, inmate,' he said, using a jovial
authoritarian tone and I matched his humour with a salute.
Then I disappeared into the shelves, folded myself between
pages that were lined with mildew, and I started to write.

THE MAINE MURDER MYSTERY CHANNEL
EPISODE 240

Release date: August 2015

Billy: Hello, listeners, and welcome to a fresh episode of *The Maine Murder Mystery Channel*. We took a little break from our live recently, but we're back on it this month with Miss Caroline Geel and all things Hotel Chrillon.

Liv: That's right. We've both been hardcore following the case – us and everyone else in the state–

Billy: And out of state, right? At this point Geel is like, national news.

Liv: And are any of you surprised? The woman shoots a man in cold blood in front of a room full of people, now we're months in and police still can't find a motive. What the hell is that about?

Billy: I've also heard that the judge presiding over the case has reservations about proceeding at all, if they can't find a motive for what happened.

Liv: That absolutely cannot be true.

Billy: I mean, yes and no, right? Because if they can't find a motive then it's a senseless crime and I'm not saying she should be released for that, obviously, because she might just go ahead and do it again. But surely, if they can't find a motive and it was senseless or whatever, mightn't that mean a psychiatric facility is on the cards?

Liv: Funny, because Geel has been seen by no fewer than two medical experts at this point too. Obviously, we're not privy to what those experts have found, if anything, but the case itself in terms of media coverage is still about as muddy as it was back in May.

Billy: Wait, I only have reports from one doctor seeing her?

Liv: No, no, it's definitely two. The defence and the prosecution, they've both had people assess Geel now, and I think, don't quote me on this, listeners, but I think they're looking to send more people in, too, to try and find a motive and stuff.

Billy: Shall we start a write-in? Listeners, we're going to pop a poll at the end of this episode, right?

Liv: Billy...

Billy: Liv, come on, there *must* be theories out there. We'll pop a poll at the end of this episode, and we want to hear what *you* think Geel's motive might have been. Answers on a postcard in time for next month.

CRIME AND CULTURE
EPISODE 152

Release date: August 2015

Aiden: Hello and welcome to a new episode of *Crime and Culture*, and this month I'm delighted to say I'm joined by a very special guest, so you won't have to listen to me talk to myself for an hour. [Laughter] For this episode, I'm joined by psychiatrist and court consultant Dr Mathew Ellis. Dr Ellis has been a working psychiatrist for some twenty years and during that time he's worked at some of the top mental health facilities not only in the state, but in the entire country. Dr Ellis has also been an acting court and police consultant during that time, too, working on specialist cases and providing expert testimony when and where it has been called for. Dr Ellis, thank you so much for joining me this week.

Mathew: Thanks an awful lot for having me and please, call

me Mathew. Dr Ellis makes me feel like I'm still on the clock. [Laughter]

Aiden: Understood. Mathew, you're joining us this week to talk about the hot case of the moment which, of course, is the Caroline Geel proceedings. Have you worked as a consultant on this case, professionally?

Mathew: I absolutely have not, no. If I had then I wouldn't be able to be here. So, everyone should keep in mind that I haven't met Miss Geel, nor have I performed any sort of assessment on her. Anything we say here is strictly conjecture based on what's available in the media at the moment. Though, there is *a lot* available in the media.

Aiden: Absolutely, there is, and thank you for being clear about all of that. Let's start with the media then, as you've already mentioned it yourself. Why all the coverage, do you think? What is it about Caroline Geel that's got everyone... I don't know how to phrase this exactly... What is it that's getting everyone quite so caught up, do you think?

Mathew: [Pause] The world has always been a little captivated by the violent offender, hasn't it? Going back centuries, you can trace human nature's interest in the topic easily enough. But I think, from my experience directly and from research I've conducted, there's something special about a violent woman.

Aiden: Special?

Mathew: Interesting, alluring, confusing. We're talking about a woman who, seemingly unprovoked, shot a man to death, in such a way that it made a spectacle of the whole affair, too. I think the concern here, and the thing that keeps all of us glued to our respective news channels, is that, if it can happen just like that [audible snap of the fingers] to one woman, then can it happen to others? So far Geel hasn't really explained why she did what she did, so we have no context for the crime, and that adds to this social unrest, doesn't it? It adds to the worry of, if one woman can do it, can another? Is this the start of some kind of uprising? [Nervous laughter]

Aiden: I'm sorry, are you trying to imply that there's something patriarchal at play here?

Mathew: [Pause] I don't think that was my intention, no, but [pause] there's certainly no reason why that couldn't be a working theory for what happened.

CHAPTER EIGHTEEN

It was the first time I'd seen Lucas in anything that resembled casual dress, and I didn't like the idea that he'd stopped making an effort. He came to see me wearing pale mustard chinos and an off-white shirt that he'd left unbuttoned – no tie, no pinstripe. The shirt looked of a decent thickness, as though if I were to pinch it between my finger and thumb it would have the same feel as good quality printing paper. For the whole of our meeting, I managed to resist the urge to lean across and validate that suspicion, even though the temptation to touch him was strong. It wasn't a sexual thing. Only that I couldn't remember the last time I'd felt human touch, beyond someone putting handcuffs on me, or Ma shaking me awake for a mealtime, which was something she was doing with a startling regularity since I'd started working on the novel again. While my appetite might have been fierce in the weeks after Noah, I found that something about writing again looked to be feeding the part of my brain responsible for generating hunger signals. If I could have been left alone with my growing stack of yellow paper, all day and every day, I would have been pleased. It would have been a greater pleasure still if every now and then someone would come into the room and rub their palm softly against the back of my bent neck in a caring, encouraging gesture – but I'd drawn the line short of asking Officer Friendly for such favours.

I rested my hand flat on the table, only inches from Lucas's own, as the meeting was drawing to a close. I'd be lying if I said it wasn't an unspoken invitation on my part. I saw him glance up and give my hand what I thought was a quizzical expression, before he cleared his throat and started to pack away his paperwork.

'Do you have any questions before we draw to a close?'

'When will I see you again?' I asked without thinking, and I hated the need in my voice.

Lucas and I had covered the details of Dr Ronan's report – by which I mean, he told me she had the beginnings of a character profile coming together, but she'd requested further visitation – and he'd warned me there would likely be another visitor soon, too, though he didn't say who. I'd already had a brush with an opposing psychiatrist – Dr Melay – who was working for the prosecution, and I had dutifully told Lucas the inner workings of that meeting. He'd asked a cluster of questions, many of which were similar to Ronan's own, and then scurried from the room like a cockroach who'd heard the hiss of a repellent spray. I didn't have much to say about the man, other than that he didn't seem very thorough. Lucas also told me that he was still conducting interviews, reading witness statements, and looking for loopholes – he didn't use that exact phrase, but that's what I took to be his meaning.

'I don't know, Caroline,' he flashed a sad smile, 'there's a lot of work to be done if we really want to try to get you out of here.'

I nodded and stared at the table. 'Why do you want to?'

'It's my job to,' he answered quickly, and I wondered whether this was a question he'd faced on the outside walls.

'Caroline, I don't understand what happened with you and Noah Prescott, if anything...' I opened my mouth, though I didn't know exactly what I planned to add, and Lucas held up a hand to stop me. 'But there's a burden on the State to prove that you are guilty of murder, so as your attorney, there's a burden on me to dispute that. Besides, I love a challenge.' He lightened his tone for this last part. 'I'll be back to see you again when I have something, but until then you should stay safe, use the wellbeing services if you need them, enjoy your privileges.'

My head snapped up at that final point and I caught his raised eyebrow.

'I hear that you have access to the library now?'

I shrugged. 'A girl has to keep busy.'

'You're not drafting a confession that undoes everything I'm doing, are you?'

I managed to laugh. 'I'm not writing a confession, no.'

'Good. In which case, I'm glad you're finding ways to keep busy.' He snapped closed his briefcase. 'I'm out of the country for the next couple of days but I'll be back early next week. If you need anything you're still welcome to call me or my office, but there may be a delay in me getting back to you, just so you're aware.'

'Anywhere nice?' I couldn't help but ask.

'Quebec.' His tone said everything. 'I'd rather not, but it's a friend's wedding.' He rolled his eyes. 'Why anyone would want to get married is beyond me,' he laughed, 'but they've been together a long time and they've decided it's, I don't know, it's time.' I cherished these moments, when Lucas revealed snippets of himself. 'Anyway, that's another story and perhaps not best shared here.' He stood from the table and smoothed down his shirt. 'Let's get you back to Ma.'

I'd told Lucas about my budding friendship with the woman who spoke as little as I did. My vow of silence had broken now, but only selectively. I spoke to Ma and I spoke to Officer Friendly, and I answered the other guards when spoken to. Beyond that, it was Lucas and only Lucas – and here he was, leaving me. I had so many questions about the wedding, the planned flight paths, whether he was taking a carry-on only or whether he'd planned to take more. I wondered whether it was a bond with Lucas that I was feeling, or only an untethered bond to the outside world. Is this place finally getting to me? And the question chased itself around my head like a rabid dog for the rest of the day, long after Lucas had gone and a pleasant enough officer had led me back to the cesspit quarters that were my home now. Not for the first time, as I wandered back into my cell, I wondered whether I mightn't have missed some key elements when thinking this whole scheme through.

'Everything okay?' Ma asked, later in the afternoon.

I was lying in my bunk, inspecting the ceiling. 'Do you ever miss the outside?'

She laughed. 'Every day, girl, every day.' I heard the creak of our shared bunk then and felt Ma's movements beneath me. Seconds later, she stood with her head level to my own and I turned to the side to get a distorted view of her. 'Struggling?'

I managed a nondescript noise and then added, 'There are things I miss.'

'Like?'

'Like looking out over my back garden with my morning coffee.' I laughed. 'Like my morning coffee.'

'Like saying "Morning boys, how's the water?" whenever I see the kids in the street.'

I frowned. 'Is that a David Foster Wallace reference?'

Ma let out a curt laugh. 'Like reading.'

She didn't seem likely to be a Foster Wallace fan, but I loved the character detail for her. 'You ever use the library here?' I asked.

'Girl, I've been in and out so many times I've read through it.'

'You never re-read?'

She shrugged. 'Once you've done a story, doesn't seem there's much to add.'

'I don't know,' I rolled my whole body over then and propped myself up on an elbow to get a better look at her, 'I think there's something to be said for revisiting a story and learning things you missed the first time around.'

Ma narrowed her eyes. 'Maybe that's your trouble.' I frowned at the comment and waited for more. 'Maybe you're too keen to go treading over stuff that's already been trod down.'

'I like redrafting.'

'But you can't always change what's been done.' Ma touched my head lightly then, brushing something away from my forehead with a mother's hand, and for the first time in weeks I thought of my own. She'd been calling Lucas and I'd been promising him I'd call her back, but like a child caught guilty of stealing more than her share of something, I couldn't stand the thought of what the call might involve. 'You need some outside world, girl, before you go crazy with this place. Use your phone call,' she added, as though she had a window into my thinking, 'get yourself some contact.'

I waited until just after dinner, when everyone was full of their meagre slops, before I went to queue for the telephones. The line was full of tearful mothers who were waiting to say goodnight to their children; a tale as old as time, the jailbird edition. I was stuck behind a woman who had said goodnight no fewer than three times and I couldn't decide whether she was speaking to a child reluctant to let her go for the night, or whether the goodbyes had been said to three different children. It was almost enough to warm a woman's heart – if I'd had an ounce of maternal feeling in me. She turned to apologise after she hung up the phone and that's when she burst into tears. I managed a thin smile and rubbed her upper arm in what I hoped was a caring gesture – and a gesture that wasn't going to get me shanked, because I wasn't altogether sure yet on what the rules were about touching other women.

'Thank you,' she sniffed, 'that's yours now.' She moved to walk away, but then turned back, as though remembering something. 'You're the one that shot that man, right?'

A layer of panic started to fold over itself in my stomach. I nodded.

The woman returned my gesture and rubbed my upper arm instead. She managed another thin smile, then squeezed. 'I bet the asshole was asking for it.'

Only he wasn't, I thought, but didn't say that because there are certain things you can never admit aloud.

I snatched at the phone and punched in the number before I could change my mind. I was pleasantly surprised that I still knew it by heart; muscle memory, from the years gone by. I'd been worried that things like that might have slipped down the scummy shower drains by now. But when the familiar dial tone kicked in and the number rang out I knew I must have it right – that, or I was about to connect with a complete stranger, which at that point I think I would have accepted all the same. An uncertain voice answered the phone – 'Caroline?' – and a wave of relief that I didn't know had been brewing hit me with the force of a winter storm against a sea wall. I suddenly understood the woman ahead of me having cried her eyes out when her call was over – and I didn't even have the tenderness of motherhood to attribute it to.

'Thank you for answering.'

The voice was uncertain; I wasn't altogether sure that there wasn't a shake in it. 'I didn't know whether you were ever going to call.'

I huffed a laugh. 'I wasn't sure whether... Look, I need to see you.' There was a long pause then, the dead air of someone breathing and thinking hard at once. 'I know it's an ask, but I'm starting to drown in this place, and it would really help if–'

'Yes,' came the pebble of an answer, 'yeah, look, of course. Of course I'll see you. How does this work? What do I do?'

CHAPTER NINETEEN

The visitors' room was new terrain for me. I took tentative steps in, like a dog arriving at a new home where it doesn't yet trust its owners, and the woman behind me hurried me along with a gentle shove. The tables were already populated with bodies, and I watched on as women I didn't know flocked to their loved ones. There were hugs and tears and harsh words from the guards who reminded people that touching was prohibited. I looked around for the table that was mine and then I spotted him, stashed away at the back of the room, half-heartedly waving as though he hoped I might not actually recognise him in the sea of it all. But of course, I would know the man from a mile away.

While Joel wore the veneer of a professional suit well enough when the occasion called for it – that occasion being singular, and that occasion being work – outside of that he was the all-American ideal. He was nearly a foot taller than me, broad in the shoulders, with a smile that would make even the hardest of hearts soften slightly; a lone dimple tucking up his mouth more one side than the other. His blond hair had lightened, I thought, though it wasn't until I got closer to him that I realised it was strands of grey coming through; platinum, stylish enough not to bother him. He was wearing faded jeans, a lumberjack shirt with three buttons undone, low enough to reveal the highest parts of the tattoo that I knew covered his chest, along with boots that made it look as though he was about to tackle a mountain. I wondered whether that was how he felt. Meanwhile, I was wearing a beige ensemble of State-issued, low-quality fabric, and shoes that I ordinarily wouldn't have been caught unconscious in, such was their resemblance to Crocs. But, knowing that Joel and I were about to see each other for the first time in months, I had managed to shove my way to the front of the shower queue that morning, so at least my hair had lost the chip-shop covering of grease that I'd been ignoring for a week before this.

I smiled tiredly when I spotted his wave and started the walk over to him. I ignored snatches of conversations along the way – 'What do you mean, she's doing drugs again... How can she not have had the baby yet... Are you seriously ending things with me during a jail visit?' – lest I heard anything I wanted to write down. Now the writer had taken over, I found it was the only salvation I had. And jail chatter was ripe with material that, though it wouldn't suit *this* book, it might definitely suit the next, or a future one. But I didn't want to be distracted when Joel and I got to talking. I wanted to be meek, mild, tortured by jail time – someone Joel might feel inclined to help.

I sighed with relief when he was close enough to hear it. 'I can't even hug you.'

He laughed. 'Imagine a hug.'

I sat opposite him at the table and Joel, forever the rule breaker, reached over and squeezed my hand.

'It's so good to see you, Caroline.'

'Please,' I tucked a strand of loose hair behind my ear, 'I look a mess.'

'Don't be ridiculous. This isn't a fashion show.' He laughed again then and pulled his hand away. 'How are... That's stupid, I'm not going to finish that. But are you okay? Are you... Are you coping?'

I shrugged. 'Coping is probably the word for it. I'm okay, I'm safe. I'm making friends,' I said this last part with a laugh on its fringes. 'Her name is Ma and she's in here for assault, I think, on her daughter, though it all sounds fairly justified.'

Ironically, Joel looked as though I'd slapped him. 'Are you for real right now?'

I murmured. 'We share a cell.'

'Fucking hell, Carrie.' He pushed a hand through his hair and looked around the room. He was the only person who'd ever called me that, and I hadn't heard him say it in so long. 'This is... Caroline, this is fucking wild. What the hell happened? Why did you... Had Noah *done* something to... I mean, were you...'

'Just ask.'

'Why did you kill him?' He spat the question out with such force that the family cluster on the table next to us turned. The woman's husband – partner, at least, from the way they were staring longingly at each other – looked truly horrified, and I wondered what his other half was in for. 'I'm sorry, I should have lowered my voice for that.'

'It's not like people don't know,' I consoled him. 'But I can't talk about the case.'

'You can't even... explain?'

I couldn't *explain* even to the people who were fighting my corner, and Joel, despite being here at my request, definitely wouldn't be in my corner on the outside. I knew I could count on Joel as a good character witness – that much he'd demonstrated already with everything he'd said to Lucas. But what I couldn't trust Joel with was information. I knew anything shared here would inevitably be spilled across a pool table later that day, or that weekend, when he was telling his friends about the wild shit his estranged wife had pulled.

I shook my head. 'I really can't. I'm sorry.'

'Then...' He looked around the room and made an effort to lower his voice again. 'Carrie, it's not that I'm not happy you called, but why am I here? What can I be doing?'

'I just...' I blew out a stream of air as though I was steadying myself – trying to put up the façade of making myself look more nervous and vulnerable than I actually felt, which I needed Joel to buy into. 'I just missed... life.' I tried to make my voice crack, but I couldn't pull it off. 'I miss the world out there, and I wanted contact and to see how you're doing, and to see what they're saying about me.'

'You're sure you wanna know that last part?'

That last part was *all* I wanted to know. Lucas steadfastly refused to tell me, only saying instead that it wasn't my concern or it wasn't anything to worry about, variations of that same tune. But the local papers at least must have blown up with the news of what had happened, and I was desperate to know whether it was widespread.

'I have to know, Joel. When I get out, *if* I get out, I need to know...'

'They're saying... They're saying a lot, Carrie. They're saying you're crazy, obviously,' he huffed a laugh, 'you shot a man, after all, so that's a standard thing for them to be saying. They're saying an awful lot about Noah, about how he must have been a bad guy, or he must have done something. The people, the people who saw you, who saw what happened, they've been on the news a lot. So has your lawyer by the way, that guy is a talker.' I felt a turn of something in my stomach even though I wasn't altogether surprised; I'd known all along that Lucas wasn't defending me out of the goodness of his heart. 'Some people are saying you must have problems, like an actual,' he whirled his finger in circles around his temple, 'like an actual condition. Then there are people who are saying it's a feminist killing,' he laughed as he said that, 'which I'm going to assume it isn't?'

I shook my head. 'I can't–'

'I know, I know,' he held up a hand to stop me, 'but there are a lot of theories going around. I think some people have even taken it up as a challenge, you know, to work it out before you confess to a motive, or before the trial or... I don't know, before the truth comes out, or something.'

'What people?' I leaned back in my chair. 'Newspapers?'

'Newspapers, podcasts, one or two YouTuber types.'

'YouTube?'

'Carrie,' he gave me a look of disbelief, 'this is kind of global.'

I bit back on a smile. 'Everyone is talking about it?'

'Everyone is talking about you, yes. I've had to fence journalists since this circus started. Honestly, it's a wonder they haven't called the goddamn jail.' Joel fiddled with one of the buttons on his shirt; a nervous tic. 'This place isn't right for you, Caroline, you shouldn't even be in here. Fuck it, you *should* be in here, because you... Carrie, you really can't talk to me about it at all? About why it happened?'

I feigned a sad expression. 'I really can't, Joel, I'm sorry. But I'm glad to know what's happening outside, what people are saying.' I stretched my leg beneath the table and took care to make sure my shoe knocked against his. 'It helps to know what's happening out there.'

'Okay, well,' he dropped his hands to the table as though in defeat, 'what's happening in here? You said you made a friend, right? That's a good thing, I think. Is there stuff to do, are you... I don't know, are you climbing the walls, or are you keeping busy?'

When I called Joel and asked him to visit, I knew he'd be an easy way of smuggling information in. Much easier than Lucas was, at least. But I also knew that he was a good way of smuggling information *out*. In the same way that any jailbird confession of mine would end up strewn across a pool table, I knew anything else I had to say probably would as well, which meant I had to take care how I answered everything in the twenty minutes we had left together.

'I have library access,' I told him. 'So at least I'm managing to read.'

'Jesus, imagine you not being able to read,' he joked, 'I'm glad you have that.'

'And,' I pulled in a deep breath, 'I'm writing.'

A louder laugh erupted out of him then and it left a wide smile in its wake. 'Of course you're writing! What is it, a prison exposé?'

'No,' I kicked him softly, playfully, under the table again, 'it's a novel.'

'Yeah, a new one?'

'Well, I started it before... before,' I said and he nodded in understanding.

'What's it about?'

'This is so cringey.' There was nothing cringey about it, but I rubbed at the back of my neck and avoided his gaze as though I really believed in what I'd said. 'And it's terrible, terrible timing, but it's a crime novel...'

CHAPTER TWENTY

To my surprise, Joel and I spoke regularly in the weeks after that first visit. He didn't suggest coming to see me again – in his defence, the jail wasn't somewhere I would have elected to spend time, either – but at the end of the visit he did say, 'Call me,' as though we were finishing up a first date and he was trying to be nonchalant about arranging a second. But given that Lucas hadn't visited, nor sent an update of any kind, Joel became the only worthwhile contact I was having – outside of Ma, whose own case had ramped up to a new level of interesting when her daughter, the one she'd hit and wound up in jail because of, then wound up in jail with us. It was a tale so laughable that I only wished I'd thought to write it myself, but I knew that wasn't where my focus could lie. Instead, I shifted my attention to Joel and everything he could tell me about the world beyond those concrete walls – which was a lot, in the average conversation. They were also conversations that came to include the daily headlines that were written about me. Despite the contents, it did wonders for a woman's ego.

We were well into August when I floated the idea of him doing a favour for me.

'What do you need?' he asked, his voice heavy with nerves.

'Do you remember Cooper?'

'Cooper? Sure, your agent, right?'

'Right.' I tucked myself closer to the phone set fixed to the wall and lowered my voice. 'This new book is coming together well and, it's been so long since I told him anything about it, and–'

'Woah, Carrie, hold the phone a second there. Are you sure about this?'

'I only want him to know how the book is doing.'

There was a long pause before Joel answered. 'But, do you not think... I'm trying to say, maybe... Do you not think there's a chance he maybe *isn't* your agent anymore, after, you know, everything that's happened?'

'He would have told me.'

'How?'

'Through Lucas.'

'Okay, and would Lucas have told you?'

Then I paused. Would Lucas have told me? Up until then, I hadn't even entertained the idea that he wouldn't have done. He's the one who stressed about us having a relationship that was built on trust – when it came to him asking me questions, at least – and the only thing I'd hoped for in return was that I'd get honesty back. But– *fuck,* would Lucas have told me? The question was angry, tearing around my head at speed and knocking other thoughts over in its path: Is Lucas on my side? Is Lucas only in this for the attention he's getting? What happens if Cooper *has* abandoned me in my hour of need? I forced out a long breath that spluttered into the phone receiver.

'Joel, I can't even think about that right now. I have to believe he would have.'

'Okay, well...'

It crossed my mind then that this was a step too far for Joel. I should have waited for another handful of phone calls to pass; better still, maybe I should have just waited for Lucas to come back to me. But my longing for Lucas's visits was starting to make me feel like a desperate Stepford who had been locked in the basement of her marital home, just waiting for the husband – or the lawyer – to peer back in. I needed to feel as though I was being proactive in his absence. I had to believe there was some way to puppeteer it all still.

'Okay, fine, fuck it, sure,' he said in a rush then and a sigh of relief burst out of me, 'if you give me his details then I'll give him a call.' He hesitated before adding, 'Do you want to tell me anything about the book, or...'

I couldn't help but smile at his effort. 'It's okay, he knows what the book is about.'

I parroted out Cooper's phone number and email address, known through my many recitations of them over the years, and asked Joel to tell him I was still working on the manuscript. Although work was slow, there was potential for me having a completed draft before the year was out. There was no way it would take me that long to complete, I knew. But I had learned over time that buying yourself breathing space in these matters was never a bad thing. Besides which, the first draft was due to be a hideously dirty one – and half of it was still being held hostage in my own safe at home, making it impossible to know for certain what the first 45,000 words even contained anymore. It would take work, to stitch the two components together, but *It's not like I don't have the time*, I thought as I rested my forehead against the cool metal of the telephone unit in front of me and listened to Joel reading back the details for a second time to be sure he had everything right.

'Okay, I got everything I need,' he said then, though he still sounded uncertain. 'Should he... I don't know, am I asking him to write to you? He can't exactly email. To you, or to Lucas?'

'To me,' I snapped. Joel had put that seed of mistrust there now, and I was suddenly happy to cut Lucas out of anything that might be about to unfold. 'To me is fine,' I said again in a softer tone. I whispered a sad goodbye down the line to him shortly after that and asked whether he'd like me to call him again. I knew he'd say yes, of course, but it didn't hurt to have the validation of it: the rushed answer; the quiet hopefulness in his tone. When Joel became a desperate dog, it was easy to see how I'd fallen for him once.

'I'll speak to you soon,' I said, 'and thanks again, Joel. You're a real life-saver.'

I practically heard the blush. 'Take care of yourself, Carrie.'

That's exactly what I plan to do...

In the week and a half that stretched by, I spoke to Joel another three times, and I spoke to Lucas a grand total of zero times. During the too quiet moments, when there wasn't enough noise to fill the hollow cave of my head, I imagined him roaming free and doing practically nothing to aid me. When it was loud, or when I was preoccupied, it was easier to imagine that Lucas was obsessed with the case, with me, even; working late into the evening with a neat scotch, a table lamp, and a stack of legal documents for company. That was the version of the narrative I was most fond of.

'Daydreaming again?'

'Avoiding your daughter again?'

Ma was leaning in the open doorway of our cell as though guarding territory.

'Please, girl, that child knows better than to show her faces.'

'Faces?'

'Mhm, she's got two of them all right.'

A laugh hiccupped out of me. 'I like that.'

'Take it. Put it in that book of yours.'

I was sleeping with a growing mound of papers underneath my pillow by then and it hadn't gone unnoticed. Ma was supportive of the fact that I was a writer still, jail not yet having taken that away from me. 'There are certain things they can't rip out of a girl, you hold onto that,' she'd said when she'd first spotted me reading back over a day's work. I felt like I was holding onto that, too; it might have been the soundest advice anyone had ever given me.

'I'll credit you in the acknowledgements.'

'You'd better.'

'Post delivery.' Officer Friendly appeared on the border to our protected lands.

Ma didn't offer to move for him. She couldn't take to the man, she'd said more than once, no matter how many favours he dished out to every inmate. Though it had occurred to me that that was perhaps *why* she couldn't take to him. Ma was naturally suspicious of people. She'd lived a life that explained that though, from what I'd heard.

'Ma,' he said as he handed her a letter, 'and Geel,' he spoke over Ma's head and handed out another letter that I couldn't reach from my bunk. Ma snatched that one from him, too. 'I'll wait and see that that's delivered.' He flashed her a tight smile.

Ma turned and handed the letter over. 'Thank you,' I said to her and then again to him, 'Thank you.'

'All in a day's work,' he said as he walked to the point of his next delivery.

'He's got a hand in every woman in this place.' Ma turned and threw her letter on her bunk with a casualness that suggested she both knew and didn't care for its contents. 'Who's writing to you, girl?'

There was a UK postage mark on the front of the envelope

and I forgot how to breathe for what felt like nearly a full minute. I pulled in a greedy mouthful of air as I ripped open the lips of the paper and yanked the letter free.

'It's just something from back home,' I answered as I unfolded the paper with hands that had developed a slight tremor. I was grateful Ma was looking the other way.

> Caroline,
>
> Thank you so much for getting your husband to contact me. I was grateful for an update from him and more than anything else I was glad to hear you're okay. I've no idea what's happening over there but your name is in lights in the UK right now. You're not exactly a pin-up for good behaviour, but I'm sure that comes as no shock. Joel said you had some reservations about our working together still so before anything else I want to remind you that we have a contract that means we keep working together as long as terms aren't broken and despite it all, they aren't, or at least I can't see a way that they are. Which means we need to start an action plan. Starting with a new book. I'm glad to hear there's one in the works because believe it or not there have been no fewer than three publishers asking questions about a story from you, whether you're writing and the rest of it. I'll be frank, Caroline; I think they're expecting a confession or a memoir. But I've told them very clearly that you're a fiction writer and that it's fiction you're working on and there's very much still interest in that, too. So be realistic with me about this book and about when it's going to be possible for me to even see it. Don't give me any of your games about when something will or won't be ready. Straight talking now Caroline, because things could get big. Tell me everything and take care.
>
> Cooper

TALK TRUE CRIME TO ME
EPISODE 384

Release date: September 2015

Darla: Hello, bookworms, and welcome to *Talk True Crime To Me*, a podcast that talks about all things true crime [pause] except when we don't [laughter]. I have a little plot twist for y'all this time around because my co-host – say hello, Eddie–

Eddie: Hello, Eddie.

Darla: My co-host who thinks he's hilarious has *rescinded* on his hot take from a couple of episodes ago, and he's going to explain why.

Eddie: I feel no shame about this. I know you expect me to feel shame, but I don't. A few episodes ago, for those newcomers, Darla *forced* me to read *Road Rage* by Caroline Geel. The same Caroline Geel who shot and killed a man, for no fucking reason, it seems, earlier in the year. Anyways,

Geel is, was, a crime writer before she became a criminal herself, and Darla over here wanted to read the woman's book and I'm going to throw my hands up and admit that it was a fucking good book.

Darla: It really was.

Eddie: And *since* that episode, Geel is still in prison, rightly so, may she rest there forever, she's *still* in prison, but it's hit the news in the last week or so that she's actually writing a book whilst *in* prison, and not only that, but some dumb fuck is planning to publish the book. Like, it isn't even written yet and there's already this wild bidding war happening around the story. So–

Darla: So Eddie asked if we could read another Caroline Geel novel.

Eddie: I feel no shame!

Darla: [Laughter] And rightly so, right, because we definitely aren't the only people picking up this woman's books these days. Her sales have gone through the fucking roof, it's outrageous. And we're contributing to that [laughter] because we've both bought and devoured *Things I Have Learned,* which is about a teacher who is selling drugs to the kids at her school, and a kid ODs from something he's bought from her. And...

Eddie: And it's a fucking good book.

CHAPTER TWENTY-ONE

It was the first time I'd seen Lucas in a plain suit. Dark charcoal with a light grey shirt underneath, even though the temperature had soared inside the jail's thick concrete. I couldn't help but imagine the sweat patches that must be forming underneath each armpit. He was wearing a thin black tie to finish, and he was fiddling with it nervously when I walked into the room. I turned to Officer Friendly to remove the cuffs for me and made a show of rubbing my wrists when I faced Lucas, feigning discomfort. He was wearing a stern set expression, and I hoped seeing me in what looked like mild pain might soften him, but–

'This shit show is everywhere.'

He threw a print-out of a newspaper headline on the table. I was too far away to see what it said, but I could take an educated guess. There were other papers lying around already, too, and I thought he must have smuggled this in among sheets of questions and printed out copies of legal loopholes. I didn't know exactly what Lucas kept in that briefcase of his, but these two things were the only items I'd ever seen or imagined him whipping out.

I collected up the paper as I pulled out my chair and took a seat at the table. Lucas remained standing; a clear indicator that I had crossed a line, and he was about to make sure I knew it. The newspaper headline KILLER SECURES BOOK DEAL FROM JAIL didn't seem like the sort of thing that would evoke pride in him, though I couldn't help but feel a twinge of it myself.

'I *haven't* secured a book deal,' I answered.

'Caroline.' He started, but paused to run a hand through his hair and then down over his face. He looked exhausted, and I almost felt a pang of guilt for whatever it was that I'd been putting him through. 'Who went to the press with this, do you know?'

'Joel.'

'And you're certain about that?'

'Who else would it be?'

'You,' he answered plainly, his voice thick with accusation. And it struck me how funny it was, that this was the thing that had tipped him over the line even though he'd long ago given up asking me why I'd murdered a man in cold blood.

'I wouldn't even know how to contact the press.'

'Please,' he yanked out his own chair and sat, 'they're drooling at the prospect of speaking to you. It wouldn't be an effort at all to get one of the snakes on the phone.'

'Okay, well, this wasn't me.' I pushed the printout back towards him as though washing my hands of the whole thing. 'I've spoken to my agent, and there's interest in the book I'm working on. I told him I have to speak to you.'

He narrowed his eyes. 'You started the book prior to the crime?' he asked, and I nodded. 'The book isn't about the crime?' I shook my head. 'Off the top of my head I don't know of any reasons why you can't still be liaising with your agent while you're in here. You aren't profiting from the crime.' He huffed a laugh then, and tugged at his tie as though he were trying to loosen it, but the knot was so tight that it didn't budge. 'Well, you *are* profiting from the crime because people are reading your other work, which I'm sure your agent has mentioned already.'

'He hasn't, actually,' I lied, 'but it's good to know.'

'You aren't profiting from *this* crime, though, and that's what the law prohibits. You won't be able to write about what you did to Noah. But given that you'll hardly talk to *me* about what you did to Noah, I can't imagine you're planning a tell-all memoir of it any time soon.' His tone was barbed, but I took the pointed comment on the chin. He was right. I wasn't planning a memoir about Noah, or anything else. I had no interest in talking about the crime anymore; in fact, it was treading dangerously close to being a source of actual boredom. But I didn't think admitting that aloud was likely to help my case, or Lucas's efforts at crafting something like innocence for me.

'I'll pass that along to my agent. He's in talks with publishers.'

He gestured to the paper front. 'So I gathered.'

'Lucas,' I tried very hard to make my tone match my intended speech, 'I'm sorry if I've caused you any additional grievances. That wasn't my intention, and of course, when I told Joel that I was writing and that I wanted to speak to an agent, it never occurred to me that that would be information he'd share with the bloodhounds of the media.' *Lie, lie, lie.* In Joel's defence, I thought but didn't say, on account of not being totally stupid, he hasn't spoken to the press; he might have spoken to someone who then spoke to the press. Either way, though, he was the perfect beard in this situation and I intended to shift as much blame onto him as I could. It occurred to me that I could force a tear or two, to really show my disappointment in my estranged husband who I thought was helping me out of the goodness of his heart. But Lucas knew me well enough by now, I thought, and a tear might tip the performance over from believable into painfully obvious bullshit. 'I'm sorry,' I said again, to seal the delivery, and then I stared hard into the table and waited for my punishment to be doled out.

Lucas sighed, and from the corner of my eye I saw him shift the paper out of view. 'You don't know what a circus it is out there, Caroline, but you... I just think you need to be careful. I understand Joel being a confidante, but he evidently isn't a trustworthy one. Leaking information about the books, I can handle him doing, but if he were to leak information about our case—'

'I know nothing about the case.'

'Well, that's partially what today is for.' He swapped sheets of paper around, reached into his briefcase to put the newspaper clipping away and replaced it with a fresh yellow pad. I bit back on the urge to ask whether he might keep that printout for me, for when this was all over. It seemed like the sort of thing I'd like framed in an office. 'I want to ask you some questions, and I want some straight answers. Can we do that?'

'I can try.'

'Okay, well try hard. If you get the answers wrong, I'll tell you what the right ones are.'

I nodded, slowly, not quite sure I understood the aim of the game. But I didn't feel as though I was in a position to push back. 'Okay.'

'Do you accept responsibility for what you did to Noah Prescott?'

I hesitated before answering. 'Yes? Insofar as I understand that I am responsible for what happened to him.'

'Do you regret it?'

No. But that's not the right answer, is it? 'Yes.'

'Well done.'

I smiled. 'Right answer?'

'It's the only answer I need.' He paused to make some notes and then looked at me again. There were small pillows of tiredness beneath each eye, and for all my scepticism about Lucas and his reasons for working on this case, I couldn't help but feel the tiniest measure of sympathy for him then, too. 'I've arranged for another mental health specialist to visit you later this week. He isn't a psychiatrist, but I'd wager that he'll be asking you similar questions to the grounds you've already covered.'

'Are there right answers I need to have ready for that?'

Lucas smirked. 'No, I think you'll be fine with this one.'

'Is it someone who's on our side?'

'The point of these people is that they don't take sides,' he smiled, 'but yes, he is.'

It had been a learning curve to observe how many people didn't instantly hate someone for having murdered someone else. I'd expected there to be calls across the State to lock me up and throw away the key, and I'm sure there *were* those calls, on the outside, but Joel, Lucas, Dr Ronan, none of them had defaulted to judgement despite knowing my dealings – and despite not knowing the reasons behind those dealings. I don't know what kept them going. Whether it was idle curiosity or proximity to the monster, or perhaps a heady mixture of the two. But Lucas looked at me like I was still a human being, not a several-headed Medusa who might swallow a man whole, and there was a certain type of magic to being able to look at someone like that, even though you were also aware of a vein of something like evil running through them. I was past the point of wondering what this whole thing said about me by then, and I was inevitably drawn to what this softness or curiosity about others. Perhaps everyone was a monster, in their own way.

'Caroline, are you still with me?'

'Sorry,' I shook my head to brush away thoughts that

belonged to the book, 'sorry, I was miles away. I... I'm just tired, I think, and this is all so much to take in still.'

'I know.' He spoke softly, and I thought in other circumstances it was the sort of tone that might be accompanied by a hug, or at the very least a friendly hand-hold. 'I know it's a lot to take in but, seriously now, media aside, guilt aside, I have a plan here, okay?' I wasn't looking at him as he spoke, but he ducked his head into my eyeline to catch my attention and I managed a weak smile. 'You have to trust what we're doing.'

We? 'You have people on my side?' I only wanted the validation. 'Despite...'

'Despite.' He nodded. 'I have people who want to help you, yes.'

I frowned. 'Help me how, though?'

Lucas looked at me as though he thought the answer was obvious. A beat of silence passed between us, eye contact only, and then he shrugged. 'To help get you out, of course.'

CHAPTER TWENTY-TWO

One of the many officers whose names I still hadn't taken the time to learn – though from his demeanour I'd already made an educated guess that he was sleeping with Ma's daughter – came to collect me from my cell four days after Lucas's visit. He didn't give me context, only said there was someone there to see me *again* – he leaned hard on the word so I could be sure it was a deep inconvenience to him to have to do his job and take me to the interview room – and then he cuffed me before starting the long walk through the halls. I was stumped when we walked right along the corridor where the private visits usually took place. He turned and nodded me along still, encouraging me towards the green space that lingered beyond the walls of the jail. I had a blissful image of him taking me outside and turning me loose, as though perhaps he was *so* inconvenienced by having to do his job these days that he was planning to let the jail population dwindle through poor management and misguarding. But alas, I was having no such luck. When we stepped into the open air of the gardens, disconcertingly quiet without prisoners to populate them, I saw that this was where I was to have today's meeting.

'He asked for you to be brought out here,' the guard said, sensing my confusion, or perhaps seeing some of it in my expression. 'I assume you've got no objections to that.' It wasn't a sincere question but a statement, or even a command, so I only kept my shoulders bunched and followed the guard to the metal picnic table closest to us, to where the man was waiting. 'Dr Samson?'

The man turned, stood, and flashed a smile that told me everything I needed to know about his monthly income. 'Oh, I'm not a doctor,' he corrected the guard, who looked suitably embarrassed by the blunder, 'just Mr Samson, but you're welcome to call me Sven.' He said this last part to me. I smiled, but not in greeting; more because I enjoyed the implication that I could be on first name terms with this man, while the good officer lingering next to me still had been relegated to the formality of a surname. 'I think we'll be fine out here for a while, officer, thanks.'

'Watch yourself,' the guard said lowly, as he turned away from me. Sven must have heard, though, because I saw him narrow his eyes at the comment.

'Caroline, I– do you mind if I call you Caroline?' I shook my head. 'Do you mind taking a seat, having a chat with me?'

I shook my head again. Though it occurred to me I might actually have to talk to the man at some point, too. He cocked a leg over his side of the bench and settled back into where he'd been sitting before. There was a strip of sunshine spotlighting the table and I was glad to settle into the warmth of it. The heat was still overbearing inside the jail, but the natural heat of sunshine against skin was a comfort despite it. I took a seat on my own side of the bench and rested my cuffed hands on the table between us.

'I'm sorry I can't do anything about those.'

'I'm getting used to them,' I answered, even though it was a lie. But I thought there was something dejected and downtrodden about the response, and I wagered that might be a façade that went in my favour. 'Sven,' I looked up at him then and his eyebrows raised at the sound of his name, 'you aren't American.'

He smiled, a softer expression this time, no teeth. 'Neither are you.'

'No.' I took a hard look at the sad landscape around us. 'No, I just wound up here.'

'Have you been in the country long?' he asked.

'Too long,' I huffed a laugh, 'if someone could smuggle me onto a plane heading for the UK right about now I'd take it. Or anywhere, for that matter. Anywhere else would do.'

'You have family at home?'

I nodded. 'My mother.'

'It can't have been easy to leave her.'

'We aren't close,' I answered without thinking.

'How's she been, with everything that's happening?'

'Like I said, we aren't close.' I avoided his gaze. I didn't want him to see anything in me that was best left undocumented. That's when it occurred to me that he wasn't taking notes. There was nothing for him to take notes with, even, and I wondered whether there was a wire strapped beneath that loose-fit T-shirt he was wearing. It was a black top paired with jeans and brilliant white sneakers; they were bright enough for me to have noticed them on the approach minutes before. Really, the guard should have been able to tell from appearances alone that we weren't dealing with a doctor. 'I've spoken to her just once since all of this started.'

'I see.' In my peripheral vision I saw him nod. 'Is there a reason for that?'

'I can't stand the questions.'

'What questions are they?'

I looked off into the distance as I answered, for the theatrics. 'About why I did it.'

'You must be sick of people asking that by now.'

'Are *you* going to ask?' I turned in time to catch his head shake.

'That's not what I'm here to talk to you about.'

'Then... what?'

'I just want to talk to you about... you. Tell me about life at home.'

I rolled my eyes and laughed. 'Are you searching for an answer in my childhood?'

'Do you think I'll find one there?'

I thought back over the same details I'd given Dr Ronan weeks before. I wasn't sure whether I could parrot them word for word, but I knew that I could paraphrase – and I also knew he wouldn't find anything of interest there. I didn't kill Noah because I'd had a poor childhood. I ran Sven through the basic timeline of it all, up until the point when adulthood hit and everything became complicated, because no one needed to hide my parents' ailing marriage or my father's escalating depression from me anymore.

'Were you and your dad close?'

'Not so close that he didn't want to kill himself,' I huffed. 'And before you say it, I'm only too aware that that's not how mental illness works.'

'Well, it's good that you know that. But you're still allowed to have feelings about what he did.' Sven left a deliberate pause, and I held eye contact with him for a moment during the space. He had an uncomfortable stare, though, not quite as comforting or welcoming as Lucas's, and I felt a twinge of disappointment in myself at having to look away first. 'You must miss him.'

I shrugged. 'I don't think about him, really.' It was true. I didn't. I wasn't sure that I'd thought much about Dad at all since the day he came home in a small casket, which my mother lovingly stored in the bay window of what used to be their marital bedroom. I remember wondering whether a man's worth of ashes weighed the same as a man's worth of body. But I shook the thought away then; it wasn't safe to get too caught up in the detailing. 'I don't think it's healthy to think about it too much.'

'Do you feel like you ever really processed it, though?'

'Oh please.' I laughed, a genuine laugh that I couldn't help. 'Are we really doing this?'

'Doing what?' Sven smiled. 'We're only talking.'

'We're not. I'm talking, you're analysing. You want to know how I felt after my dad decided that life wasn't worth living, and I'm going to tell you that I never spent much time feeling anything at all, and then you're going to force me to–'

'Woah, hold on there,' he held up his hands in a defensive gesture, 'I'm not going to force you to feel anything, Caroline, and I'm not going to force you to talk about it either.' His expression softened, as did his tone, and I realised that I'd let my mouth run too far away from me in the minutes before this. 'What happened, after your dad died?'

I narrowed my eyes at the question. 'Nothing happened.'

'Life just carried on?'

'It does, doesn't it?'

For so long I'd believed that life was a series of habits. We naturally wake at the same or similar times most days. We carry out our work duties, we come home, we make dinner, we go to bed. There is the friend whose turn it is to always buy the wine; the daughter whose duty it is to manage the prescriptions; the dog who is always walked at the same time. This, I thought, was what made death so difficult for most people to manage their feelings around – despite it being the only thing we're promised from the second we emerge from our cocoons. Dad dying, it had been a change in habit; it had been not checking he'd taken his tablets and not asking how he was feeling and not making sure he'd showered that week. Instead, it meant asking Mum what blood pressure medication she was taking and what her plans were for the weekend, whether she needed company; it was carving an hour out of every Friday afternoon to visit the garden centre down the road from her house, where we would drink tea and see what plants had been delivered for purchase that week. Life was only habitual, it had never been anything else, and death was only a rupture.

'Caroline?'

My attention snapped back to Sven then. What did I miss?

'Do you need a minute?'

'No, sorry,' I shook my head lightly to brush away Dad, 'I'm here.'

'You were telling me that you were the one who found your dad, after he passed?'

I was? I frowned. 'I don't think I want to talk about that.'

'Okay,' Sven answered, as simply as though I'd said I didn't fancy chicken for dinner, or I didn't like the colour of his jumper. Okay, like we weren't dealing in matters of life and death. 'Would you mind if we talked about Noah?'

I smiled. 'Of course, let's talk about Noah.'

I had nothing to say about Noah, that much I knew. But at least that made this safer terrain...

CHAPTER TWENTY-THREE

There was a chorus formed of rowdy inmates and disgruntled guards. Their tones blended into indiscernible sounds that made it impossible to determine who was being given what instructions, and who was resisting them. I was waiting in line for what passed as porridge – or oatmeal, as they called it here – when the rabble started. It had been a heavy writing day the day before, which meant I wasn't hungry at all. But I had learned during my time in jail already that you were never foolish enough to turn down something you were being offered. So like a good jailbird, I had decided to go to breakfast whether I wanted the meal or not. The dining room soon became a landscape of dancing monkeys and roaring things though, the latter of whom were wielding their batons and trying to herd the hungry back to their cells. I kept as still as possible as the rest of the room unfolded around me; it felt as though they were following a script I hadn't been given the pages for.

I felt a hand grab at my elbow, jerking my bowl along with it, and I turned to see Ma.

'Lockdown, girl, even for you,' she said before yanking me towards the doorway. There were clusters of bodies everywhere that made it impossible to navigate the space, and I was grateful for Ma's firm hold on me. She'd moved her grip from my elbow down to my hand, and she held it vice-like, how a mother might hold a child inside a busy shopping centre. 'Don't let go, girl, okay, because if I lose you...' She didn't finish, but I felt somewhat warmed by the implied sentiment. Anyone would have thought she was fond of me.

I'm not sure how long it took us to get back to the sanctuary of our own cell, but Ma was out of breath when we got there. She dropped herself onto her bottom bunk, rested her elbows on her knees and heaved air back into her body. Meanwhile, I lingered in the doorway and watched the hooligans still rushing from one side of the open space to another. When I glanced around I saw that some of our neighbours were doing the same as me, hovering, watching it all, and I wondered whether that made this the respectable end of the cell block – whether we were the curtain-twitchers of a jail lockdown.

'What's happening?' I asked without looking at Ma. I'd heard her breathing slow.

'Lockdown, told you.'

I rolled my eyes and turned. 'But why? Does this happen sometimes?'

'Inmate!'

I heard the holler and turned by instinct, but I quickly realised the shout hadn't been directed at me. It was so hard to tell, in a building where every woman was stripped of anything distinct: no names; no personalised clothing; no presence. There was a guard chasing down a woman I didn't recognise. When he finally caught her, he began guiding her with some force, pulling and then pushing her along when he finally managed to get her in front of him. She didn't belong on this end.

'Something happened in one of the cells.' Ma lifted her legs onto the bed and tucked both hands behind her head, assuming the position I so often saw her sleep in. She closed her eyes as though she'd given me a full explanation, and I had to bite back on the urge to go over and shake her to attention. I wasn't prone to panic, but this had caused something in me to rest on its haunches in preparedness for... anything, everything, I wasn't sure what. I only knew that fight or flight had been massaged awake, and in here I didn't have anywhere to run.

'Is everyone okay?' I asked.

Ma made a noise. 'It's only rumours.'

'In you get, Geel.' A guard appeared at our front door then, ushering me back two steps so he could tick us off his mental list and lock us down. 'We gotta get things sorted out here.'

'Get what sorted?' I shouted, though I didn't exactly expect an answer.

'Rumours,' Ma spoke again and I turned to her, 'but rumour has it someone died.'

'That's... dreadful.' It seemed a massive understatement, but I knew it was at least in the right vicinity as responses went. 'Was someone sick? Christ, could *we* get sick?' I asked, another wave of panic crashing into the wall of my stomach.

Ma laughed. 'No, girl, someone got killed, so rumour says.'

Fucking hell. I swallowed back bile before it could trespass into my mouth. It had been so easy to forget, until then, that there were women in those walls so much worse than me...

There should have been an internal investigation happening. There should have been police, detectives, cordoned off areas and witness testimonies. I knew all of this now, having lived it. But somehow, the jail had become exempt from these standardised practices. The lockdown had lasted the rest of the day and part of the next. But after that we'd been released back into the wild of the concrete jungle, with little to no clarity about what had happened, and even less information about what the jail's governor planned to do about what had happened. It felt as though in a startingly British manner, the guards had each taken their share of the weight to lift a State-sized carpet up while someone else neatly swept a woman's death beneath it. They'd dropped it with a gust of air, brushed off their hands and gone back to business. And people say I'm the one who doesn't deal with death properly, I thought as I queued for breakfast again, as I had done the day before, and the day before, and...

Ma was right when she said there were rumours. There was no margin for error when it came to the reality that yes, a woman had died. But the how and the why remained a mystery, explained only by the twenty contradicting versions of events that moved around the jail like rattlesnakes, shaking out their mis-truths as they went – only to morph into another animal, another whisper of "truth", to circulate the prison on the next hour.

'I heard she was strangled.'

'I heard natural causes.'

'I heard one guard say someone did it with their bare hands.'

I took my portion of oatmeal to a corner table where no one else was sitting and ate in peace, and as near to quiet as I could find.

'I heard it was suicide.'

When my bowl was empty I threw it into the open mouth of the wash bin that was waiting for cutlery, crockery and slops, and the smell alone caused me to pause and wonder why the fuck anyone would elect to do that job. There must have been some perks to working in the jail's kitchen, but I was struggling to see around the antisocial hours, the hideous customers and the cleanup. Still, I shouted my thanks to one of the hairnets who was standing behind the counter. If I was brushing elbows with a killer, I reasoned it probably wouldn't hurt to start being more polite. Not that many people had given *me* that courtesy.

'Coming outside?' Ma asked as I walked past her, clearly heading in the opposite direction.

'I've got a call to make.'

'Suit yourself, girl.'

I wouldn't normally call anyone at this time of day. The snake of the phone queue was akin to the outside of *Next* on a Boxing Day sale, only without the promise of discounted knitwear at the end of it, but I found myself joining up anyway. While I waited I panted crooked breaths, in and out for numbers that were at odds with each other, and by the time I reached the front of the line I couldn't be altogether sure what was exhale and what was in. I punched in the number as quickly as I could before I lost the irregularity in my lungs and then when the dial tone kicked in I held my breath entirely. By the time Lucas had answered the phone, I felt as though I'd been underwater for longer than a human should ever be able to stand.

'Caroline, Jesus,' he said when he heard my jagged hello, 'I've been going out of my mind here. Something happened at the jail?'

There'd been no way for me to know what information had leaked out and what had been censored. I felt certain the lockdown couldn't have been a complete secret, but whether Lucas knew the whys of the matter had been a mystery until now. I lowered my voice to a whisper, which only made it sound that bit more haggard when I explained.

'Lucas a woman *died*,' I rushed out, 'she was *killed*, in *here*.'

'Fuck,' he said under his breath, but the phoneline seemed to magnify it. 'Are you okay, are you safe?'

I managed a laugh, though it sounded more like a whimper.

'Safe? I'm locked up with a murderer in here, Lucas, no one... There doesn't seem to be any headway at all on what happened or who did it and they're not... There's no news, there are no police.'

The irony hadn't escaped me. And there came a long pause then that made me think it hadn't escaped Lucas either. I only had to hope he was too much of a gentleman to point it out.

'I can't stay in here, Lucas, it isn't... I don't belong here.'

'I know, Caroline, I know.'

I imagined him running a hand through his hair, then doing that thing when he rubbed his finger and thumb into the corners of his eyes; a marker of stress.

'Look, I've spoken to Sven, and I've spoken to Dr Ronan extensively, and I can't tell you everything right now, but I will, soon. We have a plan, okay? There's a plan, and we're working on getting this whole thing wrapped up without a trial even, so you just need to trust me.' I felt my back straighten as I swallowed each word like a small pill of sugar. Without a trial? 'Caroline?'

'Yes, yes I'm here.'

'Can you trust me?'

I left a deliberate pause. 'Yes, I... I think I can trust you.'

'Keep your head down, okay? Keep your head down, mind what you say to people, and I'll be in touch as soon as I have this worked out for definite. Okay, Caroline, can you do all of that for me? Just... keep out of harm's way.' He said it like he cared, and I liked that.

'Thank you, Lucas. Thank you. I don't know how I'll repay you for this.'

Though of course, Lucas had already had his pound of flesh. I'd given him a star role...

TRUE CRIME FEMINISTAS
EPISODE 60

Release date: October 2015

Hallie: Hello and welcome, my loves, to our latest episode of *True Crime Feministas*. I'm Hallie, and I'm joined here by...

Hayley: Hayley!

Hallie: And today we're talking about the latest and greatest from the Caroline Geel case, and by Christ, if there isn't some news for us to thrash out today. Lucas Williams, Geel's attorney, has held a press conference about the case this week and we are *stunned* by the comments he's making. Right, Hayley?

Hayley: I'm just going to come out and say it; I would be a lot less offended by Williams if he were a woman. Like, this whole story would read a little easier to me if Geel's defence was coming from someone who *actually* knows what it's like to be a woman in a world where men are constantly threatening you.

Hallie: Okay, first off. It's not a story [awkward laughter], it's real life. But I 100% take your point. Listeners, in case you didn't catch his statement earlier in the week, here's a little snippet for you all now...

[Muffled audio] Caroline and I have worked closely together to determine what really happened in the case of Noah Prescott's death. She isn't denying it, nor has she ever denied it, but in a world where women are constantly facing the violence of male perpetrators, I would caution members of the public against judging Caroline too harshly for her actions – actions which she has since told me she regrets, deeply. Caroline's behaviour–

Hayley: I love how he keeps saying "behaviour" and "actions" when what he's really talking about is her having murdered someone [awkward laughter].

Hallie: And that's what you're offended by?

Hayley: No, I... Well, I guess I'm offended by the implication that it's cool for a woman to go and shoot a guy for no apparent reason because *other* men are violent, and I don't like that being mansplained to me, either. I feel a bit like I'm being gaslit into thinking what she did was okay, when it definitely wasn't.

[Long pause]

Hayley: [Laughter] You straight up don't agree with me.

Hallie: I don't *dis*agree with you. But I do also think the man has a point, right? Men have been committing senseless acts of violence against women for a *really* long time, for *no* good reason, and getting away with that shit.

Hayley: But an eye for an eye–

Hallie: The world is already blind to what women go through! An eye for an eye is a flawed argument. Besides which, we have *no* idea what Noah Prescott was like behind closed doors. He kept a kid from her, for Christ's sake. What else might he have been hiding?

Hayley: Well... [Awkward laughter] It's going to have to be something pretty shady for me to agree that he should have been shot, Hall.

THE CRIME AT THE HOTEL CHRILLON
EPISODE 10

Release date: October 2015

Julie: Hello and welcome back to *The Crime at the Hotel Chrillon*. I'm joined by my glamorous co-host Sally and, such is our way, we're going to be talking about the most recent news around the Caroline Geel case.

Sally: I honestly feel like we're stuck on repeat [laughter]. Is anyone *not* talking about this case right now? Lucas Williams is a *master* media manipulator, and all I'm hearing is that the man has a plan, but no one seems to have a clue about what it is?

Julie: Someone from the DA's office did recently leak that there'd been a meeting between the defence team and the State team though, right?

Sally: Okay, sure, but can you trust a leak?

Julie: We have nothing else to go on.

Sally: The *leak* hasn't given us anything to go on! We know that there was a meeting, sometime in the last week or so, and that's literally it. I feel like Williams is a writer on a second-rate soap opera and he's just slowly drip-feeding us all cliff-hangers as the weeks go by, when all we really want to know is whether the woman is getting outta jail or not.

Julie: Well I think you can probably stop worrying about them turning her loose on the streets. It's not like there'll be *no* punishment for what happened, there's just this weird, greyscale question mark about what the punishment will be.

Sally: Life in prison, there's an idea.

Julie: You're bringing a lot of rage to the show today [laughter].

Sally: Look, I'm just... I'm sick of this not being an open and shut case. The woman killed a man. What other variables do we even need to consider?

CHAPTER TWENTY-FOUR

Lucas splayed the paperwork in front of me. He stayed quiet for a full thirty minutes while I read from the top of each page to the bottom. I was tempted to start over, too, to make sure there was nothing I'd missed. Though it was plain in black and white: Lucas had made a deal. But it was a deal so good that I couldn't help but wonder what information was missing from those pages. There had to be something that had gone unspoken, undocumented, because otherwise–

'What do you think?' he eventually asked.

'I don't understand why the DA would agree to this.'

He shrugged. 'He knows when he's up against something he can't beat.'

'And that's what this is?'

'That's what I am.'

I liked this shade on him. Lucas was renewed, as though coming back from a losing streak with the biggest of wins. He was wearing a black suit again with a thin pinstripe, a white shirt and a black tie. I wouldn't have been at all surprised if he'd paired the look with boxing gloves. He had too much energy to sit, even, and instead he was pacing the short distance from one edge of the table to the other, while I studied his offerings.

'What do you say?' he asked then. When I looked up I caught a cocked eyebrow that was borderline flirtatious. 'Do we have a deal?'

I nodded. 'I think so.'

It took more time still for the court date to roll around. The judge was a busy woman, after all, and I saw immediately from the DA's face that he was a reluctant opponent. He eyed me with a look that said our time would come, as though further down the line the opportunity might present itself for us to have a second round in the ring. Not that I'll make the same mistake twice, I thought, as I shuffled myself to an angle that meant I could easily avoid his stare. The courtroom was uncomfortably quiet bar the mutterings between Lucas and the associate he'd brought with him; an equally attractive man named Jonathan, who I thought was likely junior to Lucas by a good ten years. The pair of them presented such a neat and confident appearance that my attraction had been instant and simultaneous, and for a minute I hadn't known where to look when Lucas introduced me to his colleague. Now, I was staring fixedly at the desk and doing my best impression of a dejected and sorrowful woman.

'Are you okay, Caroline?' Lucas asked and I'd been concentrating so hard on my façade that the question made me jump. 'Sorry, I didn't mean to–'

'All rise, please.'

We followed instructions, though the DA had been standing to begin with. His awkward shuffle stilled though, and he clasped his hands in front of his abdomen as the judge entered. I wondered whether he was having second thoughts about the deal he'd negotiated. Was he about to lose his career? To be laughed out of the room – by a woman, no less? Part of me hoped so. But a larger part still hoped Lucas knew what he was doing when he made this arrangement, and that the proceedings would run as smoothly as they possibly could – given that all three men across the board were about to barter for a murderer to be released from jail.

'Be seated.'

The judge was stern set. She was wearing a different shade of lipstick this time – redder, bolder – and I wondered what she was doing before this, or what her plans were for after. Her hair was pinned into a neat bun that hung low at the back of her head, and her glasses were different, too, clear and thick framed. She was so fashionable – despite the gown, despite the scowl – that I couldn't help but idly fantasise what it would be like to have a conversation with her on the outside of this. For a second she studied the papers that were in front of her, even though she must have read them as many times as I had, if not more, in preparation for this blessed day. She turned a page, cleared her throat and then looked between the opponents: in the blue corner, the well-dressed, well-paid, high-ranking criminal defence team; in the red, the DA who looked to be shitting himself now the judge was actually in front of him.

'I hear we have a plea to make,' she started. 'Mr Tolbin?'

'Your Honour, Mr Williams and I have talked extensively about Miss Geel's case and situation, and we are both in agreement that there is evidence to suggest a contrary accusation might be made, in place of the murder charge.'

'So I see,' she said, looking at the papers again. 'Mr Williams?'

'Your Honour, as the DA has rightly stated already, there is evidence in Miss Geel's favour that warrants the murder charge be reduced to voluntary manslaughter and–'

The judge held up a hand to stop him. I tried to account for her small mannerisms: the twitch in her right eye from tiredness or stress; the way her mouth turned up at one side in that moment, as though she might be ready to laugh the deal out of the courtroom.

'Miss Geel.' I flinched at the sound of my name in her mouth. Lucas had warned me this would come, though. 'Do you accept responsibility for the death of Noah Prescott?'

'I do, Your Honour.'

'And do you feel remorse for your actions?'

I had to clear my throat before answering. 'I do, Your Honour.'

'Mr Williams, as you were.'

'Thank you, Your Honour. As I was saying, we have evidence to suggest a lesser charge would be more appropriate in this case. Caroline has been interviewed by three separate expert witnesses, two from the defence and one from the State itself, and all three are in agreement that Caroline did not knowingly cause Noah Prescott's death when she–'

'When she shot him, she didn't *knowingly* cause his death?'

The judge's tone was hard-edged. I wondered whether Lucas had overshot the strength of his argument already; got the phrasing wrong, gone in too hard, too soon. Men were forever doing that sort of thing. He should have at least allowed time for foreplay.

'Your Honour, if I may?' The DA – Tolbin, as I now knew him – requested his time on the floor, and she granted it with a nod. 'There looks to be evidence to suggest that Miss Geel,' he paused to cough, 'Miss Geel lacks mental capacity insofar as her understanding of death and its permanency. Dr Wallace for the State, and as my learned friend has commented already, two expert witnesses for the defence, were all invited to interview Miss Geel, and all three of them documented the same mental discrepancy in her view of death and dying. Dr Wallace,' he coughed again, 'Dr Wallace has delivered a report for the court, which should be in your case notes already, wherein he comments that Miss Geel's father having passed away, and her discovery of her father's body, and even the care for her mother that followed that, have had a significant impact over her perceptions of death and the socio-cultural impact that has, on both a community level and an individual one. Miss Geel–'

Again, the judge held up a hand. 'Mr Williams, your experts are in agreement with this assessment, yes?'

'Yes, Your Honour. Sven Samson noted in his report that Miss Geel exhibits a severe detachment from the concept of death, as though she doesn't quite register, as the DA has already commented, the impact that it has over the state of life. It isn't that Miss Geel doesn't acknowledge death or dying; of course, she's aware of the concepts. But the severity of these states is something that Miss Geel, according to the reports, is currently incapable of registering or appreciating.'

'This inability,' she peered over the top of her glasses, 'it's something that can be remedied?'

'With time. Dr Ronan, who also interviewed Miss Geel, and also provided the court with a report of her findings... Dr Ronan has proposed a treatment plan whereby she believes she can help Miss Geel to overcome these perceptions.' Lucas collected a sheet of paper from in front of him and read it aloud. I knew he didn't need it, though. It was all prop and gesture, all for appearance's sake. 'Dr Ronan, and I quote, "believes that a course of so-called talking therapies will help Miss Geel to process emotions relating to her father's death, allowing her time to emotionally and psychologically recover from this trauma, thereby remedying or at the very least easing the issue."'

'Easing the issue?'

'Yes, Your Honour. There is a chance this problem will persist, to some degree, owing to the time that has elapsed between the initial trauma and the present-day. However, Dr Ronan has agreed to periodically assess Miss Geel's developments in this area and report to court as and when required, to document changes in Miss Geel's state of mind.'

'It's a term of the deal,' the DA picked up then. 'We ask that these reports are delivered at six-monthly intervals, before any final decision is made regarding Miss Geel's release back into society, owing to the risk posed should this issue of mental capacity persist.'

And there it was: *mental capacity*. It was the money shot that Lucas had been waiting for, though he hadn't wanted to say it himself.

'Mr Tolbin, are you happy with the terms of this agreement?'

He hesitated before answering. 'I am, Your Honour.'

It felt like a fast and loose use of the term "happy", but the man clearly didn't have enough fight to contradict it.

'Mr Williams, given that this in your handiwork, I assume you are, too?'

Lucas smiled. 'I am, Your Honour.'

'Well,' she looked at the packet of papers again, 'I'm not altogether sure that I am.' I felt my stomach fall through me and land somewhere beneath my chair. 'We'll recess for now, gentlemen, while I review all of this in additional detail, in light of the information you've shared, and we'll reconvene later today. Thank you, all.'

'All rise.'

Lucas waited until the judge had vacated and then he pulled a twenty-dollar bill from his pocket. 'Jonathan, do a sandwich run, would you? Caroline, what'll it be?' I didn't know how he could eat at a time like this. But I also couldn't remember the last time I ate bread that didn't taste like a cereal box, so I asked for tuna and mayo on wholewheat with as much lettuce and red onion as they could possibly wedge into the thing.

Jonathan smiled. 'Consider it done.' Then he turned and fled with nothing but a brief nod to the DA, who looked to be crossing the boundary into our side of the room.

Lucas took two steps to meet him. 'I think that went well.'

'She might not agree to this.' Tolbin fidgeted with his tie. I imagined the knot sneaking higher, pressing into his Adam's apple; what shade of purple he might turn if– 'But if she doesn't, then our deal still stands.'

Our deal?

Lucas laughed. 'You're so keen to get rid of me.'

'You're damn fucking right I am,' the DA said, breaking any composure he'd had. 'I never want to see you in this State again when this is over with, do you hear me, Williams? You and I are through.'

Tolbin walked away, still fidgeting with his tie. I thought, given enough time, he might actually hang himself with it.

The judge took two hours and thirteen minutes to call everyone back to the courtroom. Though the only person who had left during that time was Tolbin – and Jonathan, once, for what he referred to as a "nervous leak" after the two-hour mark. Tolbin hurried back into the room when he was summoned, his eyes tired and his tie loosened; he didn't even bother to straighten it in time for the judge. She entered again with a few strands of wild hair and a smudge of lipstick on the left side of her mouth that made me wonder what she'd had for lunch. My sandwich was still sitting heavily in my stomach; I'd forgotten what it felt like to be full.

'Miss Geel.' It startled me that I was the first person she spoke to, bypassing the men entirely. I liked that, but I tried very hard not to show it. 'What do you make of this argument?'

I glanced at Lucas and then back to the judge. 'I'm sorry, Your Honour?'

'The argument that you don't understand death. Do you feel that way, have you felt that way, in your life?'

I nodded, slowly. 'I don't suppose I consider it much, Your Honour.'

'Did you consider it when you shot Noah Prescott?'

The question winded me. From the corner of my eye I saw Lucas open his mouth, as though to object or intervene, but I wouldn't give him the opportunity to. 'No, Your Honour, when I shot Noah I didn't consider the implications of his death, as something that would follow.' It was the right answer, I was sure of it.

The judge stared at me for what felt like an especially long time before she asked her final, damning question. 'Miss Geel, you're not going to explain to me or either of these men why you shot Noah Prescott, are you?'

'I can't, Your Honour,' I added, too quickly. Because the truth of the matter wouldn't help anyone at this stage; because the truth of the matter was only, had *ever* only been: because I wanted to know what it was like to shoot and kill a man.

The judge leaned back in her chair, shook her head and sighed. 'In which case, I'd say it's about time we called this circus to an end.'

THREE YEARS LATER...

TALK TRUE CRIME TO ME
EPISODE 452

Release date: June 2018

Darla: Hello, listeners! We're back with another episode of *Talk True Crime To Me*, a podcast dedicated to your favourite true crime reads. I'm joined by my co-host, Eddie.

Eddie: Hey, folks.

Darla: Eddie, do you want to tell people what we're talking about this time?

Eddie: Sure, okay. So, cast your minds back, listeners, three years or so, to a time when Caroline Geel was *everywhere*. You may remember an episode or two when Darla and I hopped on that bandwagon, totally abandoned true crime books in the strictest sense, and decided to binge our way through Geel's back catalogue of writing. Since then, she went to prison, blah blah, but now point a) she's outta prison and point b) she has a new novel!

Darla: Could you be more excited? [Laughter]

Eddie: I genuinely couldn't be. I was so hard against Geel after the shooting first happened, and even in that first book, but I have been *dying* for this new release, and I will feel no shame.

Darla: [Laughter] Nope, no shame at all, Eddie, I'm getting that. So, the new book, *The Girl with a Gun*, is hitting bookshelves as we speak, and we were lucky enough to get advanced copies, so that's what we've been reading this month.

Eddie: Can we start by addressing the elephant in the studio though?

Darla: [Pause] What elephant?

Eddie: Geel shoots a man, then writes a book about a woman who shoots a man. And I know what people are gonna have to say about that, *but* I'm actually gonna come out on her side here, with two points–

Darla: [Laughter] I cannot believe you're like, an advocate for this woman now.

Eddie: Whatever, I'm a fan, so sue me. The book, right, is about a woman who is slowly, slowly going off the deep end until eventually she shoots this guy, point blank on a busy street. I'm gonna say two things here. First off, Geel actually started this book way before the Prescott shooting took place. Second off, there are so many points of difference between the story and *her* story, that like, really the shooting is the only similarity.

Darla: Do we know whether her character decided to shoot a man before Geel shot a man, though? Has that been mentioned anywhere?

Eddie: [Pause] No, that has not.

Darla: Okay, well [laughter] I don't think I have anything to add there.

TEA AND TRUE CRIME
EPISODE 698

Release date: June 2018

Lucy: Hey, listeners, are you ready with your strong cups of tea? Because we have a juicy episode for you this time around on *Tea and True Crime*. [Laughter] Patrick is literally gesturing to me right now, to show he's holding a mug with Caroline Geel's face on it. [Laughter]

Patrick: I am so ready. Can we... Are we just going to dive right in with this one?

Lucy: [Laughter] I'm still laughing about that bloody mug.

Patrick: I love the merch, Lucy, what can I say? And now, I'm sure people remember all too well who Caroline Geel is, but for those who mightn't, Geel is a British woman living in the States, and three years ago she shot her lover, in a hotel bar, in front of a room absolutely brimming with people. She went to jail, she pled out, she went to prison. And now we're here, present day, she's out of prison, she's living in... I want to say Chicago?

Lucy: Chicago, right.

Patrick: She's living in Chicago, and she's just published a new novel, and I am bursting with joy about it. We managed to nab advanced copies, but the book will be available in the UK shortly and I cannot, cannot, *cannot* recommend it enough.

Lucy: The book is called *The Girl with the Gun*, because *every* crime book has a girl in the title now, even though they're always about women, and it's basically about a woman shooting someone as like, the culmination of her slowly going insane. Insane? Is that too harsh?

Patrick: I don't know that she's... I don't know that insane is right? But she's definitely slowly going off the deep end and I don't feel like we really know why, necessarily, but–

Lucy: I think it's her mum dying at the start of the book. [Pause] Wait, am I wrong? Is that not... Do you not think that's like, a catalyst for something?

Patrick: [Laughter] I can't believe you've just given away such a bloody big thing about the story.

CHAPTER TWENTY-FIVE

I didn't like New York, especially. But when you publish a book that tops the New York Times Best Seller list and your publisher tells you to pick a hotel, any hotel, no one in their right mind is likely to turn down such an offer. And I was nothing if not in my right mind: it was certified now; I had a slip of paper to prove it. Dr Ronan had worked with me *extensively* over the time I was in prison and she'd decided that we had drastically improved on the issues that had contributed towards my crime – and she was, after all, the expert. Everything had been done by the book, as Lucas promised it would be, and resultantly the State had had no other option but to release me from prison, owing to the fact that I had served my time, and I had done so under the conditions of the court.

The first thing I did when I got out of prison was leave the State. The second thing I did was a copyedit on the novel. *The Girl with a Gun* had wound up being the child of divorced parents in a publishing bidding war, where my agent negotiated what I can only describe as an offensive amount of money for a book that I still wasn't convinced was any good. Though really, I don't suppose it needed to be.

There came a knock at the hotel door, which I took to be room service. I pulled my bathrobe tighter around me and moved to answer. There was a young man waiting there with a trolley of food and a squat bottle of white wine; chilled, with condensation already running down the sides of the glass.

'Thank you, over here is great,' I said with a wide smile as I directed him towards the living area in my suite. A whole fucking suite, I thought again then and not for the first time; my luck still hadn't quite sunk in.

'Of course, Miss Geel.' He wheeled the trolley in as instructed, turned and rested his hands behind his back. 'Is there anything else that I can be doing for you today?'

'That'll be everything, thank you,' I answered as I slipped him a rolled up twenty-dollar bill. This was my life now. I had moved from pissing in front of Ma in the corner of a jail cell, to pissing in front of Louise – my prison mate – in the corner of a prison cell, to throwing around cash like I had a printing press hidden somewhere. 'Actually,' I caught his attention as he made for the door, 'I'm expecting a guest later this afternoon. The front desk should already know about it, but can you remind them, please? I know there have been some...' I lingered over the phrasing and shrugged. 'Some issues, with people trying to get up to the room.'

He smiled and nodded. 'Of course, Miss Geel.'

The man pulled the door closed behind him, leaving me to my quiet and my New York City views. The city never seemed to be still, and after the bustle of prison life there was a strange comfort to be found in occupying a landscape that always seemed to be moving. Before I settled down to eat I checked my phone one last time and found only a text from Mum – "Thinking of you xxx" – which I deleted. We were in semi-regular contact now, the occasional text, a strained phone call. My work with Dr Ronan had done nothing to repair the relationship that I now saw as desperately codependent and damaging. My mother needed too much; she always had. Her first question when I'd got my release date was when was I going back to the UK; that's also the point at which I decided I probably wasn't.

I pulled the robe that bit tighter and wandered to adjust the thermostat in the room. Then I finally made myself comfortable with my seafood platter and my large glass of wine, and I ate in a blissful silence. I read another thirty pages while my dinner settled and then I took myself to the bathroom to get ready. This room alone was bigger than the entire space I'd had to share with Louise when I was in prison. She was there for murder, too, only she got life. Apparently showing remorse can make all the difference, and she steadfastly stuck to her line that she absolutely didn't regret killing her husband, even though on the surface of it, he hadn't done anything to deserve it either. The more violent offenders I met in that women's prison, the more I wondered whether it wasn't the beginning of a crime epidemic.

I turned on my curling iron – no more rags for my fairytale curls – and I left them to heat while I painted my face. A thin layer of foundation to cover the remains of prison skin, a dryness that I couldn't shift no matter the moisturiser, and a small flick of mascara to make my eyes pop wide. I painted on a deep red lipstick, taking great care to outline my cupid's bow in a way I thought made me look more and more like the woman from the advertisement that had made me want this shade in the first place. I slipped out of my robe and hung it on the heated towel rail of the bathroom, then I pulled the black body bag of clothing from the hook behind the door. There was a splash of deep red – nearly the same shade as my lipstick – that revealed itself piece by piece as I unzipped the cover, and I felt a deep pang of satisfaction at the sight of the dress. It fitted perfectly, despite the seafood bloat from my lunch, and I took longer than I should have done to admire myself, because I had that luxury of time now. After that came the curls, the slight hiss as the heat caught still wet strands off my hand, and I slowly pulled through loose waves that fell neatly around my shoulders as though I'd staged them individually. I sprayed the look in place and then took a second to inhale, exhale, steady my breathing.

That's when my mobile hummed from the next room. It was such a shrill sound that I felt my shoulders bunch in answer to it. Sharp noises still signalled a warning in the back of my lizard brain; a hangover from prison life.

I rushed through to the living area and saw that it was Cooper.

'Isn't it hideously early there?' I answered.

'Hardly, doll, I just touched down in New York.'

'Oh, I...' I stopped, thought, tried to remember where we were in the week. 'I thought you were getting here tomorrow?'

'Don't sound so disappointed,' he answered, though I could hear a lightness in his voice, so he hadn't taken offence at least. 'I changed my flight because I couldn't be arsed with the rush of it all. I did email.'

'I haven't checked my emails.'

'You should always be checking your emails.'

There were certain parts of life that I hadn't readjusted to yet. The ability for anyone to reach me, at any time they wanted, was certainly one of them. As was the novelty of bubble baths, good food, and alcohol that hadn't been brewed in a toilet.

'I'll catch up with them now. I have some time.'

'You aren't busy then? I was wondering whether you fancied dinner.'

I rested my hand on my stomach where the food was still settling from earlier. I'd brought a renewed appetite out of prison with me. Years of enforced restriction – where everything had been oven cooked by women with track marks on their arms because of course, the women who thrived on the prison's drug supply had to work in the kitchens to gain access to it – but that restriction meant that food had become a luxury, now. I'd always thought I didn't care for it, ate only when my body desperately needed to; then, there came the hunger after Noah; now, there came the hunger for fresh ingredients. It had crossed my mind to get blood tests done, to check I hadn't brought malnourishment out of the prison system with me, and that this renewed hunger wasn't in fact my body *desperately* asking for what it needed. But healthcare had slipped somewhere down the list, after finishing a novel, arranging a book tour, and checking into a hotel that cost more a night than my dad ever made in a year.

'Caroline?'

'Sorry, Coop, I was miles away. I actually can't tonight.'

'Big plans?'

'I...' I hesitated. Cooper wouldn't judge me. That much was apparent from his dog loyalty over the last few years. But still, there was a question mark over how to explain what my evening might look like. 'I have a date,' I finally said.

There was a long pause before he answered. 'I think that's really healthy, doll. Can I ask who?'

'It's no one you know,' I lied.

'But it's definitely not a journalist?'

It was a fair question. The vultures would do anything for a headline.

'No, it's–'

There came a knock at the door that cut off my explanation. Perfectly timed.

'Actually, I think he might be here.'

'Okay, be careful. Text me when you're home.'

I couldn't help but smile. Three years in prison for shooting a man and yet, I was still at risk for going on a date with one. 'Of course.'

On the walk from sofa to door I hurried to straighten out my dress, and I double-checked my lipstick in the mirror in the hallway, too. Nothing on the teeth, I thought with a shark grin. I gave my hair one last rustle, loosening and rearranging the curls again, and then I relaxed my mouth into a normal smile – or what I thought passed for one.

And with a firm yank of the door, there he was: black suit with a thin pinstripe, fresh white shirt, but this time there was no tie.

'Do you ever not wear a suit?'

Lucas smirked and shrugged. 'Sometimes the suit comes off.'

CHAPTER TWENTY-SIX

Cooper was a mid-forties man with thinning hair and a casual dress sense that cost him ridiculous amounts of money to maintain – the clothing, that is, not the hair. He'd arrived at my hotel suite so early that he caught me in a brilliant white pyjama set, with my hair just about maintained in a messy updo. I had no make-up on and I was only halfway through a coffee, brewed to perfection by the sweet man who was now the regular server when it came to my room service demands: seafood platters; late-night pizza orders; the strongest coffee you can muster. I was sipping at the drink and staring out into the city while Cooper paced the same five steps in front of me, obscuring my line of vision. He was running through the details of the day's events and I was trying to ignore him. It felt rude of me, but not quite as rude as it was to turn up at someone's hotel suite unannounced before nine in the morning.

'I'm sorry,' I managed to tune in to what he'd been saying, 'their names are actually Hallie and Hayley?'

He looked down at the sheet of paper he was holding to fact-check himself. 'Yes.'

'What are they, children's TV presenters?'

Cooper sighed, set the paper on the coffee table and perched on the edge of a nearby armchair. 'No, they're podcast presenters.'

'Jesus, Cooper.' I sipped my drink again and left a deliberate pause. I was getting used to how people waited for me to finish my sentences now, to how people were giving me space. 'I know they're presenters, but they sound like teenagers from their names alone. They're not actually kids, are they?'

'*True Crime Feministas* has built up a really strong following over the last few years, Caroline. They even covered your case, when you were... Well, you know.'

I cocked an eyebrow at him. 'Were they on my side?'

He took too long to answer; I didn't like how long he was having to spend mulling over the question. 'They weren't *not* on your side.' Cooper sighed and ran a hand through what little hair he had left. I wanted to caution him against it. That kind of behaviour would only make it tumble out sooner. But then, working with a convicted killer probably hadn't done much for his hairline over the years either – even if it had kept him in good clothes. 'They mostly talked about your treatment as a woman in a male-dominated space. How you were treated differently to male offenders, how Lucas presented your case, that sort of thing.'

'And today they want to talk to me about?'

'I just went through this, Caroline.'

'Mm,' I sipped again, 'but I was busy trying to enjoy my allotted thirty minutes of quiet for the day.'

'They want to talk about the book, of course, your release, whether you're being treated fairly post-conviction.'

'I won't talk about Noah,' I snapped.

'And they know that.' Cooper huffed a laugh and, in a tone that I didn't like the cut of, he added, '*Everyone* knows that at this point, Caroline.'

I shot him a stare full of bad feeling. 'I think I'd like to get ready now.'

Cooper stood and nodded. 'Understood. I'm going to leave the itinerary there, and the question sheet, just in case. I'll be downstairs grabbing breakfast when you're ready.' He trod towards the door then and I stayed fixed, staring at the city outside. 'I'm on your side, Caroline, always,' he added. Though of course, I knew that literary agents were always on the side of their clients – and the money.

Hallie and Hayley weren't teenagers, though they were the type of blissful and bubbly young women that I might have crossed the street to avoid in other circumstances. Hallie wore bright red lipstick and had her brilliant blonde locks shaped to a severe bob that cut angularly where her jawline ended. She was wearing skin-tight black jeans and a loose-fitting white blouse, see-through enough to reveal a mess of tattoos across her torso and back. Hayley wore less make-up. Her hair was long, wavy and had most certainly been styled by a professional that morning. She was wearing a long black maxi dress with a slit up one side that revealed too much thigh when she sat down. I was glad I'd gone for a cream linen suit, paired with a slouchy black t-shirt beneath it; I was smart, casual, age-appropriate. Nothing made a mid-thirties woman question her fashion choices like two women in their mid-twenties, but I thought I looked like the respectable one out of the three of us, which is how Cooper liked me to style myself for these things.

We were in a well-lit studio with an audience chomping at the bit to be let in through the double doors at the back of the room. This was the first live podcast episode that the girls – *sorry, young women* – had ever done and their nerves were contagious. I felt a ball of trepidation in the well of my stomach at the thought of strangers being unleashed into the same space as us at any second, as well. It reminded me too much of prison, that flood of people, the sea of unknown faces. But I forced out a long breath and tried to find a façade that would make me at least look more comfortable than I felt.

'We'll be guiding people to their seats now, ladies, okay?' a young woman wearing all black and a headset leaned in to tell us. A fraction of time later the doors opened, and I thought I saw her flinch. 'Is there anything I can get anyone?'

Hallie answered for her and her co-host. 'We're all good, thanks, Suzi.' Then she turned to me. 'Is there anything you need, Caroline?'

'I've got everything, thanks,' I said, gesturing with a copy of my novel as I spoke. It was a hardback edition, and I wondered whether I could use it as a defensive weapon should the occasion call for it. There was quite a lot of weight in the story, after all.

Hayley held me in idle chatter while people filtered into their seats. Did I like the city? Did I know how long I was going to be there for? How was I enjoying life in Chicago? It was the kind of filler that radio hosts had given me already; so much so that my answers were comfortable, parroted. She was midway through asking me what my plans were for after New York when Suzi appeared again with a two-minute warning.

'Okay,' Hallie flashed me a wide and bloodied smile, 'we're going to be sticking to the sheet exactly; there are no surprise questions here. We'll aim to wrap up within an hour, too, so if you need to clock-watch then you can,' she said this last part with a laugh, but I was thankful for the information all the same – not least because I'd been clock-watching since I entered the room.

I side-eyed the audience and caught Cooper sitting at the

end of the first row. He flashed me a smile and a thumbs up right as Suzi started to count us into recording.

Hallie pulled in a greedy breath before she turned to face the audience. 'Hello and welcome to a new episode of *True Crime Feministas*, angels, and this episode is particularly special because we are *live* from New York City. Hello, audience members!' There came a rumble of low cheers and excitement from the bodies watching us. 'Now, we're veering away from true crime *slightly* for this episode, but I'll hand over to my gorgeous co-host to tell you a little more about that.'

'I actually thought you were going to steal my lines,' Hayley said, with laughter breaking through her voice. 'Thanks, Hall. So yes, we are live, and we're also joined by a very special guest for this episode. Now, if you've followed the podcast to date then you'll already know that we're mad on true crime and pop-culture, and this guest is a medley of both things. We followed the Caroline Geel case determinedly when proceedings were ongoing and now here we are, with the woman herself, all these years later. Can I please get a round of applause for Caroline Geel, everyone?' The audience obeyed. I couldn't decide whether it was paranoia or astute hearing, but I was convinced there was at least one boo or hiss. 'Caroline is currently touring around the States to promote her new book, *The Girl with a Gun*, so we've invited her along today to have a chat with us about that, alongside one or two other things. Caroline, good morning and thanks so much for joining us.'

'Thanks for having me,' I smiled, 'and thank you, audience members, for giving up a Saturday morning to be here.'

'I'm sure I speak for everyone when I say it's a genuine pleasure,' Hallie answered.

'Now, Caroline, I'm going to dive right in here,' Hayley started, though she paused to readjust her dress, lest she flash a member of the audience first, 'you are a highly driven, talented woman, constantly tackling very male spaces, and on a podcast that celebrates feminism and true crime, we're obviously all about that. Can we talk a little about what the publishing industry has been like, in that respect?'

'Well,' I left a deliberate pause, 'it's a little easier than prison, I can tell you that much.' There came a rumble of laughter from the hosts and audience alike. 'But of course, absolutely. I think publishing gets quite a bad write-up, and sometimes I really do understand that, but I have to hold my hands up and admit,' I actually held my hands up there, 'I've been treated with huge amounts of respect, for this book more than any other.'

'That's so interesting,' Hallie answered, and Hayley murmured in agreement. 'Is there a reason for that, do you think?'

I opened my mouth to answer, but–

'Do you think it's because your editors know you'll shoot them otherwise?' The question came from an unknown audience member; a male voice, heavy with resentment. The studio became pin-drop quiet. Hallie and Hayley looked as though they'd been slapped. Suzi was staring into the crowd trying to spot the perpetrator of the crime. And I did the only thing I could possibly think to do that didn't involve a gun.

'I think there'll be time for audience questions at the end of the episode.'

The shocked pause lasted only a second longer before a slow clap started among the audience members. Hallie and Hayley looked at me like I was a goddess among women. Suzi joined in with the stir of clapping. Cooper made an A-okay sign at me from his corner post. And I couldn't help but smile and think: Yes, yes, I've won the madding crowd around now...

CHAPTER TWENTY-SEVEN

Of course, despite the cautions delivered by the show's producers about filming segments of the recording, someone managed to sneak in a smartphone all the same. The altercation with the heckler was online before I'd even made it back to my hotel room that day, and in the two days that followed it went viral. New York hadn't exactly been an easy place to remain anonymous to begin with, despite the size of it. But by the end of that week I found that I couldn't even grab a coffee without, 'Oh my God, you're Caroline Geel. Can I get a selfie with you?' And when you're in the process of slowly winning over the public, it turns out the only appropriate response to that question is, 'Yes, of course, I'd be delighted.' My face was all over Instagram and I didn't even use it. But people had taken to tagging Cooper and my publisher's account whenever they posted a picture of me and naturally, both were overjoyed with the free publicity. Though it did make it hard for me to have anything like a day off, unless I spent the day wallowing in my hotel; which felt like a middle-class problem if ever there was one, I reminded myself as I moved from one room of my suite to another.

I was waiting for Cooper to collect me for an upcoming book launch we were doing that evening. It felt disingenuous to call it that, though, given that we'd done so many launches by then, and I was still operating under the disillusion that book launches were a one-time thing. They had been, once, and they were barely attended by a live audience back in the day either. So the fact that Cooper and my publisher had agreed to double down on security for the evening – following The Podcast Incident – spoke volumes as to how many people they thought were likely to attend.

I used the time wisely by studying myself in one of the many mirrors dotted around the room. There were too many of them, and it made it impossible not to fall into vanity. For that launch, I was wearing a black dress that cut away midway down my calves and I'd paired it with a bright red shawl that matched my book cover and my lipstick. I felt shamefully coordinated, but I was quietly proud of myself for it, too. My hair was neat in corkscrew curls, which meant it sat nearly on my shoulders, some two inches higher than it would normally have done, and the curls were fixed in place with so much hairspray that I was convinced it made me a fire hazard. I'd been gazing so intently at myself, a regular Narcissus, that I jumped when the knock at the door came.

'You scared the shit out of me,' I said by way of a hello as I opened the door.

Cooper laughed. 'Sorry, I should have got them to call up. Are you ready?'

'What do you think?' I held my arms wide and did a twirl so he could admire me.

'I think you look too gorgeous for a book launch. Let's blow the whole thing off and get dinner.' He angled himself so he could offer me an arm to hold, which I accepted. I'd paired the dress with shoes that would cripple me. 'Seriously, shall we forget the whole thing?'

I pulled the door closed behind us with a hard click. 'We both know you don't mean it.'

'Oh, but if only...'

We swapped idle chatter in the cab on the way there. Cooper took me through the itinerary for the following days. He'd deliberately pencilled in an extra couple of days off, too. We weren't going to be in New York for much longer, and he wanted to give me time to explore the city, so he said, before we moved on to the next one. He was just in the middle of telling me which sights I should visit when the car pulled to a stop and the driver announced we'd arrived. Some unnamed individual opened the door for us and I slid out first, followed by Cooper, who I knew would tip the driver on our behalf. This is my life now, I thought as I climbed the steps at the back of the bookshop-bar where the event was being held. There would be an offensive queue already out front, and Cooper tried to keep me away from that sort of thing until absolutely necessary.

'Caroline!' A woman who thought she knew me threw her arms around me as we walked through the door, and I leaned into the hug as though she were an old friend. 'I'm Dora. I've mostly dealt with Cooper so far, of course, and Sarah-Jane from your publisher's place, but I'm so, so happy to finally meet you.'

And to her credit, she seemed it.

'It's so nice to meet you, too. Cooper has told me so much about you,' I lied. Cooper didn't say a word to me about these people because he discerned early on that I genuinely just did not care about them. 'Where do you want me?' I asked with some urgency, keen to get the moving parts in place.

'Oh, right over here.'

The woman guided me by the elbow to a raised platform at the back of the bookshop. Instead of the usual line-by-line of chairs, there were small tables and squat seats, as though we really were in a proper bar, and it made it impossible to know which persona they wanted from me. She showed me to my seat, a lone perch in the centre of a too big space, and asked whether she could get me anything to drink.

'We've got time, because we're only just checking tickets for people now.'

'I'll get a–'

'Caroline will get a Diet Coke, and I'd like one, too, if that's okay?' Cooper had been talking to another member of the bookshop team since we arrived – a lesser member, I assumed, given that he hadn't thought to introduce us to each other – but he tuned in to the conversation as soon as there was a risk to be contained. He doesn't want me to drink, I realised then, so he wants *sober Caroline* for tonight's performance.

'Of course, I'll grab those right away.'

'Are you feeling okay?' Cooper asked in a low voice when it was just the two of us.

'As okay as I always am before these things.' There was a loud click of a door opening somewhere and the resultant bustle of human voices that followed. Cooper saw me flinch. 'I'm fine, really,' I rushed to add before he could ask again.

'Two Diet Cokes,' Dora announced as she reappeared in lightning speed. 'Cooper, I've reserved this front table for you, will that be okay?'

'Absolutely,' he answered without looking, though he took the drinks and passed one to me. 'And it'll be a twenty-minute reading, question and answer, book signing? As agreed.' It didn't feel like he was actually asking her, but rather reiterating a set of instructions. But in her very professional, eager-to-please way, Dora nodded along and said, 'Yes, yes,' to everything she heard. 'Great. Could I just grab a minute with Caroline to myself before we get started, Dora, if you don't mind?'

'Oh my God, absolutely. I'm just a fusser,' she laughed, a nervous, twitchy sound, 'just give me a call if you need anything, I'll be... ah, getting people seated, I suppose.' She raised her arms and let them fall heavily to her sides in a gesture that seemed the tiniest bit defeatist, and I wondered whether she'd expected to be invited into our inner circle pep talk rather than brashly excluded from it.

'Now, what do I always tell you before these things?'

I laughed. 'It'll be over in no time.'

'And?'

'And then I can have a drink.'

'Atta girl.' He winked; I hated that. There were times when I really wondered whether Cooper mightn't have been a better bet to place money on than Noah, but I guessed that ship had sailed now. 'Nothing at all that you need?'

'Only to get started.' I looked past him to the audience that was slowly filtering in, taking their seats with large glasses of wine and podgy bottles of beer. 'Do you think they'll get brave if they're drinking?'

'Caroline, look at me.' He waited until I dragged my eyes back to him. 'There is security in all four corners of this room. Nothing and no one is going to get past us this time around, okay?' He reached forward and gave my hand a reassuring squeeze. 'Besides which, if anyone does get brave, you'll only put them down on camera and it'll inevitably go viral and make you *more* famous, so, silver linings, kid.'

I laughed again. 'Thank you, Coop.'

'Any time.'

Cooper back-stepped carefully from the raised platform of the stage and took his seat then, just as everyone else finished taking theirs. I took a sip of my drink and felt the ice knock against my teeth, sending a small shock through me, and then I set it down on the table by my chair. I grabbed my book, made myself comfortable, and pasted on the nervous smile that I reserved for audiences these days. I was famous, but wasn't I humble with it...

Dora stood at the back of the audience, out of sight, and gave me an encouraging look. She cast an eye to her co-workers, to check they were in place, too, and then she held up three raised fingers to count me in to my introduction. One, two–

'Well, this is quite a turn-out,' I started, laughter breaking in at the edges of my voice. 'Thank you, firstly, to everyone who's come along this evening, and thank you as well to Beer and Books for hosting this event. I have to say, a bookshop that brings drinking and reading together might just be my new favourite place on earth.' There came a low rumble of laughter and agreement from the audience. 'I'm Caroline Geel,' I paused for my own laugh then, 'though I suppose you all know that by now. And I'm really delighted to be here this evening to talk about my new novel, *The Girl with a Gun*. I'll be doing some readings from the book to get things started and we'll be welcoming questions after that, so if you could save your heckling until then that would be great.' The laughter was louder then, authentic, and I spotted Cooper looking impressed from the front table, too. There was something to be said for turning a shit show into a PR opportunity; something I felt well-versed in by this point. 'So I'm assuming everyone knows about the podcast incident...'

While I loved the quiet of writing, mostly, there was something to be said for the instant gratification you felt from a live audience. The more they laughed throughout my introduction, the more I felt my body relax into the seat, the steadier my voice became.

'But enough about all that,' I finally said, 'you're here to hear me read from this.' I held the book up in front of me like a shield. 'This sparkly and wild new creation of my mine. I believe Dora and her team will be selling copies of the book and

I'll be signing them for you after the reading, though if you can get a rare unsigned copy it'll probably be worth more down the line,' I added, going in for one final laugh before we really got into the deep water.

I cast another eye around the room quickly, looking for the hidden security team that Cooper had made promises of. There was a man lingering at the back, arms folded, making his sharp suit pull awkwardly on his shoulders. I didn't know whether he was security, but I wouldn't have minded having him on my side in a bar fight. Then, on the opposing side to that, there was–

Lucas.

I flashed another nervous smile and cracked the book open on my first tabbed page. 'Let's get this show started then.'

CHAPTER TWENTY-EIGHT

It was another two days before the banging on the hotel door started. It was late at night and offensively loud. I was already in bed and I considered not answering, but something of that volume would stir too much interest in the surrounding suites, and I'd worked too hard to earn any bad press for myself at this stage. I tumbled out of bed, grabbed a bathrobe to throw around my nightdress, and hurried to open the door. There hadn't been a call from the front desk, to approve a new visitor or alert me to one, so I knew there was only a handful of people that it could be. And of course, it wasn't too much of a surprise.

'What the fuck is this, Caroline?' Lucas burst through the door, waving around a copy of my book as though it were a deadly weapon; an apt comparison if ever there was one.

'By all means, come in,' I said as I closed the door behind him.

'Seriously, Caroline, what even is this?' He was still waving the book around.

I trod over to the living area and stooped to collect an opened bottle of red wine from the table that I'd left there earlier. 'Do you want to grab a glass?'

'I don't want a goddamn drink.'

'Okay,' I answered as I popped the stopper out of the bottle and poured myself one. Lucas remained quiet – perhaps he was shocked by my calm – as the liquid glugged into the glass. When I'd half-filled it, I set the bottle back down and settled on one of the sofas. 'Are you going to sit or are you happy to keep pacing?'

'Don't be so fucking calm with me,' he snapped, 'this isn't an interview.'

'No,' I sipped, 'if it were then you might have a better attitude.'

He threw the book on the table and it landed with a thud that made me flinch.

'Sorry.' Lucas kneaded at his forehead and huffed a laugh. 'I can't believe somehow I'm the one apologising to you. Caroline, of all the fucking things you could have written. I *told* you not to write a goddamn confession.'

'And it isn't.'

'She shoots a man.'

'The title didn't give that away?' I snapped back, my own voice rising then. 'Sit the hell down before you blow a gasket.' Lucas followed my instruction but he took the armchair that was the greatest distance away from me, and he only perched on the edge, ready to leap up at any moment and resume his laps of the room. 'You read it quicker than I expected you to.'

'It's gripping stuff,' he answered, though it didn't exactly sound like a compliment. 'Caroline, *everything* about this book is you.'

'That's absolutely not true,' I sipped again, 'and you know that.'

'Okay, *most* of this book is about you.'

'I'm not crazy, Lucas. *She*,' I pointed to the book on the table between us, 'is crazy.'

'Caroline, you shot a man in cold blood. She–'

'Shoots a man in cold blood, I know, I wrote it. But there are extensive Instagram reviews where people have heavily annotated that book, highlighting all the ways in which *she* is not *me*.' I said it a little too smugly, given that my line of defence was hinged on crime readers across a social media platform. Of course, there had been enough people raising suspicions about the contents of the book, too, but the former far outweighed the latter. People didn't care about how true the book was. They only cared that it was a good yarn. 'I don't understand why you're making such a thing out of this, Lucas.'

'Caroline, I defended you. I argued your case, and I made a good goddamn case.'

'This book doesn't invalidate your work. That is entirely separate to this.'

'Is it?' His voice rose again. 'Caroline, this woman kills a man because she wants to know what it feels like to murder someone. Is that...' The question died out but I wasn't going to answer it without him asking properly. He'd banged down my hotel door at an unrespectable hour; the least he could do was ask what he came here to ask. 'Is that what you did, is that actually what was happening in that fucking head of yours?'

'You're asking how autobiographical the book is.'

'Yes, that's exactly what I'm asking.'

'Lucas, you've read it, you already know the answer to that.'

He ran a hand through his hair and down over his face, just like he had during our jailtime together. I'd almost missed that stressed, harried sequence. 'How much of the book is autobiographical?'

'The murder.'

'The motive?'

I took a sip of my drink and weighed up the answer. 'The motive.'

'Fuck me,' he muttered. 'You're actually–'

'I wouldn't, if I were you,' I cautioned him. *Crazy* had been thrown around a little too often for my liking over the last five years and I wasn't about to take it from him. 'You'd do wisely to remember exactly how the defence attorney behaves in that book before you go shouting about it being a true story and all.'

Lucas's eyes widened. 'I'm sorry?'

I set my glass down on the table, stood and crossed to the counter where the empties were waiting. When I was back between the many sofas I poured Lucas a large glass of red, set it on the table and nudged it towards him.

'He bribes the DA to get the charges dropped for his client. Isn't that right?'

Lucas leaned forwards to grab his glass of wine then. He took two thirsty mouthfuls, moved it away, then moved it back for another two before he set it back on the table. The glass was nearly empty. His hands were clasped together, and his eyes were fixed on the book still lying between us.

'When did you know?'

'Please,' I sipped my own drink, 'you're good, but even you have your limits.'

There was a long and uncomfortable pause then. Lucas stared accusingly at the book while I sipped through so much of my wine that I was topping up the glass by the time he spoke again.

'Does anyone else know?' he eventually asked.

'No, Lucas, it's fiction.'

'Only it isn't!' He shot up from the seat and started pacing; I knew it would happen eventually. He'd never been able to keep still when he was nervous. 'When did you... How did you even know?'

'The hushed conversation between you and the DA at the end of the trial. He wasn't just scorned, Lucas, he was outright pissed, and I knew then that there was something going on with you two. After that, I started digging.'

'Started digging where?'

'In the cold dead earth where your histories are buried.' I sipped my fresh drink. 'You two were actually close once upon a time, weren't you? I managed to find out that you even assisted him on a case back in... God, do you know, I even forget the year. But I'll bet *you* remember it. Drunk driver, hit and killed a kid, and didn't you help him to get the guy off? Didn't that same guy then go and... what was it?'

'He did the same thing again, two months later,' he answered flatly.

'That's right. Another incident, another dead kid. And...'

'And Tolbin defended him again.' He sucked in a deep breath. 'I assisted, again.'

'Neither of you did anything wrong.'

He laughed. 'Apart from setting free a kid killer.'

I shrugged. 'It's nothing you don't do now.'

'You didn't kill a kid.'

'That's right, Lucas. I didn't, and that's exactly why you defended me. I killed a man, in front of a room full of people, and *you* with help from your little buddy, got me a sweet deal. I got *myself* everything that came after it. So what's the problem here, hm?'

'I believed those medical reports.'

'You were meant to!' I snapped back.

He made another noise; it was less a laugh, and more of a defeated huff. 'They were fiction, too?'

'Everything worth believing is.'

'Accept your actual work of fiction, which is basically a fucking autobiography.' He kicked the table. 'You can keep the book, Caroline.'

I cocked an eyebrow and Lucas headed for the door. But on

the short journey, he decided he wasn't quite finished. I wondered whether it had dawned on him just now, or whether it was a question he'd been dying to ask since he got here. Maybe he just hadn't been able to look me in the face as he asked it.

'This isn't your first book, Caroline. The others...' I imagined him running a hand through his hair; that trademark gesture. 'The other books,' he forced out, 'what are they?'

I didn't turn to answer. But I did sip my drink to leave a heavy pause between us.

'I've never written fiction, Lucas.'

The door slammed shut with the force of a gunshot.

TEA AND TRUE CRIME
EPISODE 708

Release date: July 2018

Lucy: Good morning from the not-so-sunny United Kingdom! We're settling down to record today's episode on one of the grimmest days that July has had to offer so far.

Patrick: But we're only partway through the month and this is an English summer, so there's still all to play for.

Lucy: Well, regrettably there is that. But despite the shoddy weather, we're extra-extra excited to be recording today's episode for a couple of reasons. Patrick?

Patrick: That's right, because we have actually pulled out all of the stops we can muster for the episode and got [pause] a special guest joining us in the proverbial studio.

Lucy: Exactly that, folks. In a slight departure from the true crime we usually serve to you, we're serving you some sparkly crime fiction, from an author near and dear to our geographical hearts. Caroline Geel is a British born author who migrated to the States several years ago now, and she's recently been winning fans on both sides of the Atlantic thanks to her brand new book *The Girl with a Gun*, which was published earlier this year.

Patrick: For this episode Caroline has kindly agreed to join us for a chat about the book and all things crime fiction, and we're delighted to have her here. Caroline, thank you so much for agreeing to come on the show today.

Caroline: Goodness, thank you for having me. What an introduction!

Lucy: We're just so excited to be able to talk to you about this book of yours which, it has to be said, is fan-bloody-tastic.

Patrick: It really is. I ghosted Lucy for two days while I read it cover to cover.

Caroline: [Laughter] That's every author's dream, I think, to have a reader so buried in their story like that, so thank you. I'm, ah, well, I'm just really glad to hear you both enjoyed it.

Patrick: But we're going to backtrack a little before we get too caught up with this latest story, if you don't mind? Because *The Girl* is actually your [pause] fourth novel, is that right, Caroline?

Caroline: That is right, absolutely. I've been writing for quite some time now, but *The Girl* is the novel that seems to have brought everyone's attention around to the first three books I wrote. Though I think a lot of authors – that is, a lot of authors who make it big time, and I say big time with big bunny ear quote marks around it – but a lot of authors who make it to that level of interest and success, I think they often have a few books beneath them already before that happens.

Lucy: I actually said this to Patrick when we were doing prep for the show. Gillian Flynn's *Gone Girl* is the classic case of this, for me. *Gone Girl* blew up and suddenly everyone was like, hang on a minute, there's a back catalogue of novels here from this author that we haven't read yet.

Caroline: That's a great example, and a great book, of course. I think Flynn's success is a good template. Not that I'm saying *The Girl* is in any way as good or as big as *Gone Girl*, obviously, but–

Patrick: I don't know, let's not be hasty. I've got a slip of paper in front of me here that tells me sales are into the millions at this stage. Is that right?

Caroline: [Nervous laughter] Honestly, it makes me slightly nervous to even think about the numbers, but yes, I've heard that sales are into the millions.

Lucy: Which is wild in itself! Does this give you confidence when it comes to your next book, would you say? Knowing that there's such a market for your stories now?

Caroline: Who says there'll be a next book?

Patrick: Oh, come on!

Lucy: [Laughter] You will outright break Patrick's heart if you tell us here and now that you're not planning to work on another novel in the future.

Caroline: Well, look, I think when you have a book that goes global in terms of its interest, it can do two things for any writer. As you said already, Lucy, it can be the confidence boost that every author needs to sit up a little straighter and think hey, maybe I *am* good at this, maybe this next book *will* be okay. But it can also have a confidence crushing result, in that, you shrink a little at your desk and think hey, what if the next book isn't as good this one?

Patrick: [Hesitating] So, are you telling us there *is* another novel?

Caroline: [Laughter] You two don't quit!

Lucy: [Laughter] And I don't think Patrick will, incidentally.

Patrick: I really won't.

Caroline: Okay, okay [laughter]. Yes, there *will* be another Caroline Geel novel. But I'm not saying what and I'm definitely not saying when...

CHAPTER TWENTY-NINE

Of course, the more suspicious people called it a publicity stunt. There were comments across the internet to that effect. But if anyone could have heard the steaming phone call I had with Cooper on the morning that the headlines landed, they would have known that that wasn't quite the case. Newspapers on both sides of the Atlantic brandished KILLER PLANS PRISON MEMOIR and CONVICTED GUN-WOMAN PLOTS PRISON EXPOSÉ, among other things. Worse still, they had pictures in support of what my research looked like. I had foolishly thought my hotel suite was a safe haven from that sort of PR horse shit, but apparently I'd been mistaken. There were grainy prints showing stacks of books about the States' prison systems, dating back to when women-only prisons started, through until now. The only saving grace was that I'd had my notebook with me at the time the pictures had been taken, and my other additional research – including a shaky opening chapter – had been locked away in the safe of my laptop. But still, the violation was cutting, and I felt a deep burn down to my belly because of it.

Cooper was determined to get to the bottom of who was

responsible for the leak. But it didn't take a genius to work it out – and it wasn't anything to do with my years of piecing together crime narratives that helped me, either. On the morning that the headlines broke, my breakfast was wheeled in by a different waiter.

I smiled, thanked him and handed him his tip. 'Where's the old kid?' The new kid – who wasn't a kid at all, really, but someone who looked at least ten years senior to the last hotel employee – shuffled awkwardly, grimaced, and stared down at his feet. A second or two passed before he shrugged. 'I see.'

'Is there anything else, Miss Geel?'

'No, thank you, I... Sorry, I didn't catch your name?'

'Henry.'

'And that other waiter's name? The last one?'

He shuffled again, and his mouth bunched up at one side. 'Seb.'

'Seb,' I parroted, rolling the traitor's name around my mouth, greasing my teeth with it. 'Thank you, Henry.' I held out another twenty for him to take, which he did, though he seemed hesitant to at first. 'You've been really helpful.'

I called Cooper back while my tea brewed. 'There's a young man at the hotel by the name of Seb. I'd like him fired.'

A long pause came before Cooper answered. 'You're sure?'

'Mm,' I lifted the lid on breakfast, 'please.'

'I'll speak to the manager. Caroline, I'm really sorry about this.'

My scrambled eggs were wafting up towards me, but the smell did nothing to entice my stomach. 'It isn't you who needs to apologise, Coop, honestly. All press is good press, you taught me that.'

'But still, it's your fucking hotel room.'

'Suite,' I corrected him, 'and it really doesn't matter. That said, and I know we're not in New York for much longer, but–'

'Consider it done. Pack up, and I'll have you out of there by the afternoon.'

'Thank you, Cooper.'

I disconnected the call, collected my tea and a crust of toast, and crossed to the sofa that looked over the skyline. I wagered that any replacement hotel would have just as good a view, and likely just as fickle wait staff. But it would speak volumes if we changed hotels following the leak, and that was a repercussion the hotel should have to deal with.

There was only a handful of things I really needed to do before the sand on my New York City timer ran out – one of which was to see Lucas for a last time. And I guessed it would be one last time forever maybe, not just while I was in the city, given how we'd left things before. But there was another engagement I needed to keep as well.

Ma had been released from prison earlier than me, though we'd been separated from each other earlier than that, when our jailtime redirected us through different systems. She'd been kind enough to keep in touch and I found I valued that. She was based in Maine still, born and bred, but when I'd mentioned a free flight to New York she'd said that she could find both the time and the money to put herself up somewhere for a few nights. I would have offered my hotel suite, given the space it boasted, but somewhat ironically I hadn't trusted her to keep the details of it private.

Now, we were sitting opposite each other in a nice enough restaurant where both of us looked out of place, albeit for different reasons. I was looking at the menu, but in my peripherals I could see Ma scouting out the space around us, admiring the room as though she'd never seen such high ceilings outside of a State building. When I looked up she smiled at me and nodded. 'You did good, Caroline.'

I shrugged. 'This is the least I can do.'

'I don't know why you think that.' Ma grabbed at her menu and I thought I saw a gathering of saliva form at the side of her mouth as she started to read. 'I treated you the same way I treated everyone else.'

'Only, you spoke to me more.'

She laughed. 'Only because the rest of 'em can't be trusted.'

'Speaking of which, how's your daughter?'

A deeper, more authentic belly laugh erupted out of her then. I'd never heard her make that sound before. 'She's fine, girl, she's fine.'

'Still inside?'

'Out and back in.'

I frowned. 'I'm sorry to hear that.'

'Best place for her.' She shrugged. 'Though it means I'm spending most of my time playing Mama Bear to a three-year-old cub.'

'Jesus.' I looked back at the menu. 'You really did deserve a trip out of Maine.'

'Hm. Never seen New York before.'

'Can I get you ladies some drinks?' A petite and too smiley waitress appeared out of nowhere. She was wearing a short black skirt, a white shirt and red tie, and her make-up was, I guessed, just the right side of appropriate for the workplace. 'Or are you ready to order food?'

'I'll take a gin and a slimline tonic, please, ice, no fruit.'

Ma huffed. 'I'll take a beer. Whatever is on tap.'

'Okay then,' the waitress answered as she scribbled, 'and food?'

I hadn't had more than my slice of crust that morning, and I wasn't sure I could face much else now. But it hardly seemed right to invite someone to a luxurious lunch and then refuse to order anything that wasn't liquid – or alcoholic.

'I'll go for the chicken bistro salad, but can I have the dressing on the side, please?' The waitress nodded as she took down my order. 'Ma? Sorry, I didn't even ask if you–'

'I'll take the beef stack burger with fries and slaw, but can I get onion rings on the side of that, too? And what's your garlic loaf like? Texture, I mean.'

'–were ready,' I finished and laughed. 'We'll have everything she just said, including the garlic loaf, thank you.'

'No trouble.' She took our menus from us. 'I'm Cindy, and if you need anything else today then don't hesitate to give me a call.'

'Thanks,' Ma and I said in unison.

'That loaf might have the texture of ass,' Ma commented when it was just us again.

'But at least it won't be beige toilet water.'

'Ah, good times. You're doing well, Caroline.'

I shrugged. 'I turned things around.'

'Good for you, girl. I always thought you might.'

I couldn't help but narrow my eyes. 'Why's that?'

'You have that about you. I'd wager you could turn anything to your favour.' She took what felt like a deliberate pause while Cindy brought our drinks to the table. 'I'd say given enough thinking space, like that in our cell, you'd probably even find a way to make jailtime work as an advantage.'

Ma looked at me then as though she was trying to tell me something, and it took me perhaps a beat too long to work out what it was. Though deep down, I'd guessed that she might know. And a little preparation in case of these things never hurt.

'That reminds me,' I reached down into my bag on the floor and pulled out a thick envelope, 'I brought you a little something.'

Ma let out a hearty chuckle. 'Prison talk reminded you that you brought me something? There's not a shank in here, is there?' she asked as she took the package from me. I didn't answer, only dropped back in my seat and sipped at my drink while she pulled the lips of the paper apart. 'Caroline, how much–'

'Twenty thousand.' I cocked an eyebrow at her. 'Probably doesn't go far with a toddler.'

'It goes further than you might think.' She set the money on the table between us. 'That isn't why I came to visit you.'

'It isn't why I asked you to.'

'Then why–'

'I told you, you were good to me.'

'That's not a reason to pay me off.'

'No,' I lingered for a second then added, 'that isn't.'

Ma nodded. After that she was quiet for what felt like a long time; half a gin and tonic, to put a unit of measurement on it. Then she reached forward and tapped the money. 'I didn't need this.'

I shrugged. 'Take it anyway.'

In all the time we'd spent together in jail, I'd never seen Ma wrong-footed by anything or anyone. Even during the lockdown that time, she had remained cool and in control of everything that was unfolding around her. But now, she looked uncertain. I thought I could even hear the thunder crack of cogs turning while she worked out how to play the hand that I'd so willingly dealt for her. Soon, she nodded again, and collected her beer bottle from next to her. She held it towards me, as though signalling for a toast, and I matched it with my glass.

'To crime,' she said, and I couldn't stifle my smirk. 'And to getting away with it.'

CHAPTER THIRTY

It took a week and six missed calls before Lucas finally submitted and answered. I didn't have long left in the city, something that I reminded him of, and even though I'd gone into the conversation prepared to make my case for us seeing each other again, it became all too apparent, all too quickly, that I didn't need to convince him at all. He willingly agreed to it, though he did seem rumpled when I told him firstly that I'd moved hotels and secondly, that I wasn't prepared to tell him where my new one was. Instead, I suggested a restaurant with a private dining suite for their "special guests", which seemed to be another way of saying that they funnelled their celebrities into a back room to stop the heathens from taking pictures of them whilst they were eating.

Lucas mumbled. I heard the rustling of paper in the background, and I didn't like that he was splitting his attention so obviously.

'Tomorrow?' I pushed.

'You'll never get a reservation there for tomorrow.'

'I already have. I'll see you at half past six.'

The private dining area was everything that I once imagined my someday life would be, though I never *truly* imagined I might get there. A young man took my coat as I entered, a young woman took my drink order before I'd even been shown to my table, and a tall cosmopolitan was waiting for me already as my chair was pulled out by another waiter. Lucas was waiting there, too. He surveyed me up and down, cocked an eyebrow and huffed as I got settled into my seat, and then he sipped his neat scotch and said nothing until the flurry of waiting staff had disappeared. But even then, he didn't exactly say anything. Instead, what he did was reach down into his briefcase to pull out one copy after another of my previous three novels and lie them side by side next to each other, with their covers facing me. From this angle already I could see dog-eared pages and Post-it notes protruding from the edges, punctuating passages that Lucas might have thought were noteworthy. I wouldn't have been surprised if there had been colour-blocked paragraphs, too, stained with highlighter that I desperately wanted to be bright pink for the contrast it would have created against Lucas's sour face. I surveyed the covers, reached down into my own bag, and pulled out Lucas's copy of *The Girl with a Gun*, which I lay on the table alongside the others but with the cover facing him.

'You're missing one.' I tapped the dust jacket of the book. 'I took the liberty of signing it for you, with love and thanks.'

Lucas pulled in a thirsty mouthful that didn't seem to phase him at all, though the mere thought of the swallow made me wince.

'You killed your dad.'

The room immediately slowed then. Waiters were moving at half the busy pace they had been only seconds before; the muted sounds of the other diners became a white noise crackle;

and my heartbeat was a bass drum in my head. It was the type of panic I hadn't known before, despite everything I'd been through, and I wasn't altogether keen on the physiological reaction to something that, logically, I must have known would come one day. Still, it was the blunt force trauma of the statement that came as a surprise, and I found I was inwardly counting breaths then to avoid showing any outward signs of weakness to this man, this worthy opponent, who had finally put the jagged pieces of a puzzle together.

This, I quickly decided, would be one of life's many turning points that are thrown at us, during which time we have to determine at knee-jerk speed whether we'll sink or swim. And I wasn't about to drown at the hands of a man who happened to have a sharp suit and a good nose for detective work. It wouldn't be now, I decided then; it wouldn't be him.

'I *helped* my dad,' I answered, and sipped my drink to give myself a chance to breathe. 'He was sick.'

'He was depressed.'

'How is that any different to what I said?'

'Tell me what you did to him.'

I handed him the noose, I remembered as I sipped my drink again. We were going to need another round before we'd made our way through the books on the table. 'Do you have any idea what it's like to watch someone self-destruct, reassemble, and self-destruct again?'

'I'm getting a clearer idea of it, yeah, Caroline.'

'Spare me, that isn't me, that isn't what *I* do. That's what *he* did though, every year, every month for my entire life. He *begged* me on countless occasions to help him make his life easier, to help him take it all away, and I knew exactly what he was asking me every time he said that.'

'So what was so different about this time?' He tapped the

book front with his index finger. 'Why did it happen this time and not before?'

There had been nothing different about that time, I didn't think. Only that I'd said yes... 'I got sick of seeing him sick,' I admitted. 'Dad had had enough of life and I couldn't keep forcing him through something that he didn't want to be a part of. The tablets weren't working,' I shook my head and corrected myself, 'the tablets might have worked, if he'd taken them to instruction, if he'd taken them consistently, but he didn't and he never had, and every time he messed around with them he fell deeper and deeper into his own head until...'

'Until you said yes.'

'Yes, Lucas, until *I* said yes, until *I* helped. It wasn't murder. At worst, it was assisted suicide. And any other exhausted carer would have done the same thing.'

'Assisted suicide is still a crime, Caroline.'

'Not morally.'

Lucas pulled in a thirsty breath and, as though defeated on the first front, he moved a hand and tapped the second book on the pile. 'You killed someone in a hit and run.'

I nodded, but I didn't say anything. I wasn't sure whether he was hoping for a confession, further panic, or a heady mixture of the two. But now we'd ripped the plaster of the first book off, suddenly the second plot didn't seem as intimidating – nothing about this did. After all, Lucas didn't have evidence; he had theories. And he'd already proven in a court of law, time and again during his career, that theories didn't get you anywhere. Apart from the private dining area of a high-end New York City eatery, it seemed.

'When you were married to Peter still, there was a hit and run accident five miles away from where you lived. A young woman was walking home from a party late at night when a car clipped her and sped away. There were witnesses to what happened, but none that could actually name the type of car it was.'

'And?' I asked pointedly.

'And you happened to trade in your car within thirty days of that happening.'

'It was an old car.'

'A lot of damage to it, was there?'

'From age, yes.'

Lucas sipped his own drink then, but this time he did wince, the hard mask slipping for a second only before he yanked it back up over his face. 'Tell me what happened.'

I couldn't help but smile. 'It sounds like you already know what happened. But that isn't what happens in the book.'

'No, in the book a young *man* is killed on a country road by a woman who's driving late at night after an argument with her spouse. She drives away and does everything she can to cover up the crime.'

'Poor thing is in a blind panic for most of the story.'

'And were you?' I frowned at the question. 'After you hit the girl, were *you* in a blind panic?'

'Can I get you two some menus, now that the first round of drinks has settled?' It was a timely interruption from the young gentleman who'd pulled out my chair for me, two-thirds of a cosmopolitan ago. He glanced between us both and then dropped his eyes to the books splayed on the table, and his expression shifted. 'You're Caroline Geel,' he said, his tone changing from professional to excited in a heartbeat. 'Oh my God, you're actually...'

I forced a laugh, a bashful one, I hoped. 'I am, yes.'

And the waiter laughed then, too. 'I'm sorry. We meet so many people in this job and we're coached beyond belief not to react, but... My God, you're *actually* Caroline Geel.'

'Can I sign something for you?' I offered, because that was

usually how these conversations went. Besides which, I wasn't as eager as I might normally have been to brush away the attention. The kid was buying me a reprieve.

'Oh,' he pressed his hands against his chest, 'I would love that, but we're really not meant to ask. But thank you so, so much. God, I'm sorry, this is so...'

I waved away the rest of his sentence. 'Nonsense.' Then I reached into my bag for a pen. I pulled out the napkin from under my drink and scribbled, "From Caroline with love", followed by my autograph, and then folded it over to cover the crime. 'Consider it a tip for such good service,' I said as I pushed it along to the table's edge.

'Thank you,' he gushed as he took it and slipped it into his pocket, 'thank you, so much, and I'm so sorry for interrupting your drinks.' He said this last part to Lucas, who had the decency to smile. 'I was asking about menus.'

'We'll take another round,' Lucas answered then and he turned to me to add, 'but we won't be eating.'

'Of course, absolutely. I'll be right back with those.'

Lucas laid books one and two on top of each other. 'Two kids died from an overdose at a school you worked at in the UK.'

'Hm,' I thought back, 'if memory serves right, another kid was found guilty of having supplied the drugs to them.'

'And where did that kid get the drugs, Caroline? Was it you?'

I narrowed my eyes. 'You don't think a teenager would have cracked and admitted that to someone at some point, rather than taking the heat all by themselves?'

Of course, I knew that wasn't exactly the case.

Joseph stayed quiet about where he'd got the drugs for the same reason that all kids keep crucial information to themselves: he was a teenager in love. I hadn't slept with him, because even to me that felt as though I would have been crossing a line. But he and I made wild plans with each other – to run away, to start anew, to wait until he was a real, live boy old enough to live out the dream of fucking his teacher – and those wild plans were enough to encourage him towards putting money anyway, towards helping me keep my little sideline going right up until the moment when two of his peers took everything too far. I hadn't thought about him in years, not really anyway, because what reason was there for me to think of him at all? Now, if he were to tell the truth to anyone, he'd be a low-level drug dealer trying to make a name for himself by piggybacking on the name of his former teacher who happened to be famous these days. And even that wasn't a real concern. First, given that he'd kept quiet for this long, it seemed unlikely that he'd go running to the police so many years later. Second, Ma had already shown me the ways in which money can, in fact, buy happiness and freedom – and silence. There was no one left for me to worry about now about apart from–

'Jesus Christ, Caroline.' Lucas slapped his hand flat on the table and the noise brought me back into the room. 'I don't know what kind of power you have over people, or even how you have it. All I know, all I *think* I know right now, is that you're leaving a paper trail of murder behind you on both sides of the Atlantic and I'm the bastard that helped to keep you out of prison. Is that the truth, Caroline?' I looked up at him and, strangely, I thought I saw his stare soften. It loosened to caramel around the edges of deep brown before hardening again, the black pupils suddenly taking up too much space. I wondered whether he regretted sleeping with me now.

'Ask me what the next book is about, Lucas.' He shook his head, as though in answer, but still he leaned in closer to me and lowered his voice to a hoarse whisper.

'Tell me what the next book is about, Caroline.'

Like a montage, I remembered the riotous behaviour when

the prison went into lockdown. The noise and the cattle herding and the battle cry of every inmate who felt violated by the one woman who had to go ahead and get herself strangled as soon as her cell door had swung open that morning. Every person felt affronted by the woman who'd died that day, but no one, not even the guards, seemed to care all that much about the woman who'd killed her.

I matched Lucas's lowered tone. 'It's about a woman who's murdered in jail.'

'And here are your drinks.'

'I have to go.' Lucas shot back from the table with a force that sent the drinks rocking. He dropped a twenty on the table and shot an apology at the poor waiter. 'I'm sorry, attorney at law and all that.' He forced a laugh that sounded as though someone was applying pressure to his windpipe. 'Great service, young man, truly,' Lucas fumbled with his briefcase, 'it's just a... There's an emergency.' He stared at the books that were on the table and I saw the hesitancy flicker across his face: take it or leave it, take it or leave it... 'Thanks again,' he said to the young man, before he hurried for the exit.

'Something I said?' the waiter asked.

'Not at all.' I managed to laugh then, too, though mine sounded easier than Lucas's had. 'He really is an attorney and there's been some break on a case or...' I waved the sentence away. 'Who knows. But it's no trouble at all. I don't mind drinking alone.'

'Can I get you anything else, Miss Geel?'

I looked down at the four books in front of me and smiled. 'I'll take a dinner menu actually, if you don't mind? I think I could do with a little something...'

'Of course. I'll grab one for you now.'

The hustle with Lucas had obscured my view from the back window until then. Though the restaurant didn't feel it on entry, it must have been higher than even my first hotel had been. The panoramic view of the city was enough to still my breath for a second or two. I reached across the table then to collect Lucas's fresh drink, and I took a hearty mouthful of it. The scotch swilled around my teeth, under my tongue, as though cleansing the detritus from the forced confessional. And then I swallowed hard, watched the sun dip, and actually enjoyed the burn on the way down.

THE END

ALSO BY CHARLOTTE BARNES

SUSPENSE THRILLERS:

My Husband the Murderer

A True Crime

The Good Child

Penance

Safe Word

The Things I Didn't Do

Sincerely, Yours

All I See Is You

Intention

CRIME:

The DI Melanie Watton Series

The Copycat (book one)

The Watcher (book two)

The Cutter (book three)

AUTHOR'S NOTE

In my day-to-day life when I'm not writing crime fiction, I'm a lecturer in Cultural Studies at the University of Worcester. Here, my research specialism is True Crime. Over the last few years I've given a lot of time to researching true crime narration, and how this style of writing often treads the line between the factual and the fictive. It's because of that that I felt the need to include an author's note in this book.

The seed of Caroline Geel, both as a character and in terms of her story, is borrowed from a real criminal: María Carolina Geel; birthname, Georgina Silva Jimenez. She was a Chilean writer who, in 1955, shot and killed her lover Roberto Pumarino at the Hotel Crillón in Santiago. I stumbled across this crime during work for an academic project, and though the project wasn't specifically about women who kill, I found that I couldn't shake my thoughts of Carolina Geel's case. She would never discuss her motivations for killing Pumarino, though there were *many* theories about why she might have committed the crime. Psychologists were enlisted to evaluate Geel's mental state; social theorists became embroiled in the case; there was even a school of thought to suggest she might have done it to gain publicity for her work as a writer, which had slipped under the radar to a degree, particularly in comparison to works by other female Chilean writers at the time. There has never been a definitive answer as to why Geel did what she did and of course, as a fiction writer specialising in true crime narratives, this gripped me.

It would be remiss of me, then, not to acknowledge and credit this real-life story as having been a huge source of inspiration in my own writing. Geel – my Geel, that is – has very clear and very different motivations when it comes to her criminal dealings, and in that way she is entirely separate from the real story. In many ways, though, the real-life informed the fiction, and for that I feel somehow indebted to Carolina Geel, and to Alia Trabucco Zerán, the author of *When Women Kill* (And Other Stories 2022), for alerting to me to Geel's case in the first instance. The real-life Geel hasn't been the topic of much literature, but if you're at all intrigued about her story, Zerán's work – which includes the details of three other cases from Chilean history besides Geel's – is an excellent place to start.

With love and thanks -
Charlotte Barnes

A NOTE FROM THE PUBLISHER

Thank you for reading this book. If you enjoyed it please do consider leaving a review on Amazon to help others find it too.

We hate typos. All of our books have been rigorously edited and proofread, but sometimes mistakes do slip through. If you have spotted a typo, please do let us know and we can get it amended within hours.

info@bloodhoundbooks.com

Made in the USA
Coppell, TX
20 February 2025

46172631R00141